AMISH WIDOW'S PROPOSAL

EXPECTANT AMISH WIDOWS BOOK 5

SAMANTHA PRICE

CPSIA information can be obtained
at www.ICGtesting.com
Printed in the USA
BVHW030355201021
619298BV00029B/300

CHAPTER 1

Commit thy way unto the Lord;
trust also in him; and he shall bring it to pass.
Psalm 37:5

EVELYN PUT a hand on her swelling stomach; her unborn child kicked in response, soothing Evelyn's frayed nerves. If her baby was moving it was a good sign.

She'd never expected her husband would die so young, but here she was at his funeral service held in her sister's house. Sitting amongst her community and staring at the coffin, she wanted to cry like a regular widow, but the tears wouldn't come. She might as well have been at the funeral of a stranger and not the man who'd been her husband for the last eight years. The only genuine sorrow she felt was for three-year-old Martha and her unborn child, who would both grow up without their father.

Glancing down at her hands, she noticed the deep

color of her nerve-rash, which showed beyond the edges of the long sleeves of her dress. With one arm holding Martha on her lap, she pulled her shawl higher on her neck so no one would see the ugly redness that would've traveled to her neck by now.

Martha and Evelyn had practically lived on their own, as Amos had found one excuse after another to stay at his late father's house. It had all started when Amos' mother had taken ill—he stayed back at his parents' house to help out. Then later, when his mother died, Amos stayed on to look after his father. Any normal Amish family would've moved the father in with them, but when Evelyn suggested the obvious, Amos responded that his father wanted to stay in his own house.

Evelyn had suffered feelings of rejection, which made her disconnect further from her husband. Amos spent the odd night back in the marital home, but after his father died, he still stayed on at his parents' house. Even though Evelyn hadn't been in love with him—they were married. She had hoped that another child might make them more of a family. If they had just one more child, surely Amos would see the importance of staying in their own home like a proper family should.

Her marriage to Amos had been anything but perfect, but the people she'd confided in—her older sisters—had told her that no marriage was perfect and every marriage needed to be worked at.

Evelyn glanced at her sister, Sally, sitting beside her. Sally was the nearest to her in age and had been blessed with a wonderful marriage to Mark. They were married a year before Evelyn and Amos and now they had two boys. Oftentimes, Evelyn had to fight the envy she felt over her sister's loving relationship with Mark. Why was it that God blessed some with love and withheld it from others?

Even though Evelyn had never loved Amos, she'd never considered she'd be left alone. She closed her eyes and asked God to forgive her for the times early on in their marriage when she'd wished him dead. Death, she'd considered, was the only way she'd be free of the marriage that should never have taken place.

At last, a tear trickled down her cheek. Her sadness was for Martha and her unborn child, and as the tear fell from her face the reality hit her that she was completely on her own. No man would be handing her money for the fortnightly shopping, and there would be no one chopping the firewood or fixing the old buggy that sorely needed replacing. She was now totally responsible for two young lives, and for the upkeep of two houses. Feeling alone was something she'd grown used to, but she realized she'd never been more alone. This time there was no one to blame for her problems.

She looked up at the deacon who was giving the word of God.

Closing her eyes tightly she wondered where she'd be now if she'd taken a different path; if she'd ignored the older ladies who'd convinced her that Amos would make a wonderful husband. The trouble was that all her older sisters and all her friends had married, leaving Evelyn the odd one out. She'd longed to be married and have someone to care for—someone who would in turn care for her. The ladies had been wrong when they'd convinced her that love grows after marriage.

When they'd first dated, Amos had been caring and loving, but once they were married, the affection and attention abruptly stopped. Evelyn had tried to be a good wife by keeping the house clean and cooking all the food that he liked, but nothing had ever been good enough. It was as though he'd stopped trying to be nice as soon as they were wed—he'd claimed a wife and that was one job out of the way, in his eyes.

I can't go back and change things now! She'd been blessed with Martha and soon another child would be born.

But how would they live? Amos hadn't made much money, but they'd managed to live on the money he provided—there was nothing kept in reserve.

Her husband's latest excuse for staying in his parents' house had been that he was fixing it to lease out to give them extra money to live on. Amos's motivation to fix the house was equally as slow as his work on it.

Her attention was drawn back within the room when the deacon sat, and the bishop stood up to take over. As the bishop spoke, Evelyn's eyes glazed over and she pictured the last time she'd seen Amos. He hadn't spoken of pain, although he must've been in pain according to the doctor. They'd had an argument about the kitchen tap that needed fixing. Amos said he'd fix it later and Evelyn had grown annoyed. There were too many things that needed fixing. She explained that he should take some time to hear of the things that needed repairing. He'd said he was almost finished with the repairs on his parents' house, and Evelyn challenged him; she didn't believe a word.

He walked out, shutting the door loudly, and that was the last time she saw him.

Martha squirmed on her lap, turned around, and whispered, "Finished now, *Mamm?*"

Evelyn stared back into the blue-green eyes that matched her own. "Soon, baby, soon."

Martha turned around and laid back against her mother's chest with no idea she was at her father's funeral. Evelyn had tried many times to explain that her father had gone home to God where he belongs, and they would see him again one day. Martha thought that he was simply still at *Grossdaddi's haus.*

"Are you okay?" Sally whispered leaning into her.

"Yeah, I'm okay."

Martha turned around again. "Are you crying, *Mamm?*"

"I'm not. Now turn to the front and listen to the bishop."

Martha did as her mother told her.

As Evelyn's house was small and in a state of disrepair, the viewing of the body and the funeral service was held at Sally's house. Evelyn was pleased and grateful that no one would have to see inside her house.

Amos had barely lifted a hand to repair anything in their home. No house can go years without constant care and attention, and hers hadn't had any for years and that was the reason it was falling apart.

It was all Amos' fault. He'd tricked her into marrying him by presenting a false front to her, and now he'd ruined her life again by leaving her with two children to raise with no money.

I will get through this day and then I'll figure out what to do. Evelyn wiped another tear from her eye.

Sally leaned into her and whispered, *"Gott* will help you get through this hard time."

Evelyn managed a smile. She hoped her future would be better than the past few years. Even though she hoped for a better life, she didn't deserve good in her life since she'd been so evil. She closed her eyes and asked forgiveness for often wishing Amos dead. Did her wicked thoughts have a hand in her husband's death? Did the devil hear what was in her heart and ask God to take Amos away as punishment for the foolishness in her heart? Perhaps she was a sorceress who could make things happen by merely wishing. She sniffed back the tears she felt coming and put a hand on the top of her stomach to still a sudden bout of nausea. The bishop should know the evil thoughts in her mind and in her heart. If she confessed her sin to the bishop, she might feel whole.

"Come on. Are you ready?" Sally said as she rose to her feet.

Evelyn looked up at her sister, realizing that the service was over. The songs had been sung, the words had been spoken, and all that that was left was to go to the graveyard.

Sally leaned down and picked up Martha. "You come with me, Martha."

With Martha off her lap, Evelyn was able to stand. She looked down at her large stomach, which was much bigger already with this baby than when she'd been pregnant with Martha. This baby seemed like he or she would be much larger than seven pounds.

As Evelyn walked out of the house, she heard whispers of Amos and how he'd died. She heard the word 'aneurysm,' and wondered what the people would know of such a thing. Evelyn had never heard about aneurysms before her father-in-law had died of one. Amos had died in the same way.

Martha took hold of her hand again once they were outside the house.

"We go home now, *Mamm?*"

"*Nee,* not yet. We go to the grave. Remember I told you about that?"

Martha nodded. "Goodbye, then home?"

"*Jah,* then we can go home after the graveyard and after we say goodbye to *Dat.*"

Martha looked around. "Where's *Dat?*"

Evelyn hadn't allowed Martha to see her father's body lifeless and still. She'd tried to explain that they were saying goodbye to her father today, but that was as much as Martha understood. Evelyn couldn't bring herself to tell Martha that her father was in the wooden box—the one that would be lowered into the ground and covered by dirt.

"Would you like me to drive you to the graveyard, Evelyn?"

Evelyn turned around to see Hezekiah, a widower with three young children. His wife, Jane, had died two years before of pneumonia.

"*Dat!*" Martha said, which made Hezekiah's face light up.

"*Nee,* Martha, it's not *Dat!* This is Mr. Hostetler. You know Mr. Hostetler." Embarrassed, Evelyn turned back to speak to Hezekiah. "I'm sorry; it's the beard, I think." Hezekiah had a similar-length dark beard, like Amos'. "*Denke,* but we've arranged to go with Sally and Mark."

He nodded and touched his beard. "Jane's been gone for some time. I know these next months won't be easy for you. If you need anything done around your place or with your livestock, just let me know." He wagged a finger. "Be sure to ask if you need anything."

"I will *denke.*"

He looked down at Martha and patted her on the head and Martha gave him a beaming smile.

"I think they're ready to go," she said pointing at Sally and Mark's buggy. When Hezekiah nodded, she walked toward the buggy holding firmly onto Martha's hand.

"You're hurting, *Mamm.*"

"*Ach,* I'm sorry. I didn't know I had such a tight grip."

It was a squeeze in the back of the buggy with Sally and Mark's two boys, seven-year-old Daniel and six-year-old David.

"You okay, Evelyn?" Mark asked.

"We're doing okay. I'll be glad when I wake up tomorrow and this day is behind me."

"It must be hard for you. Let me know if I can do anything to help out."

"*Denke*, Mark; I appreciate that." In her mind, Evelyn laughed. There were so many things that needed doing around the house she would scare everyone off if she named them all. Still, it was nice of people to offer.

CHAPTER 2

Study to shew thyself approved unto God, a workman that
needeth not to be ashamed,
rightly dividing the word of truth.
2 Timothy 2:15

WHEN EVELYN GOT HOME LATER that night, she put Martha to bed and pulled the covers up around her neck to keep out the chilly night air.

"Will *Dat* be here tonight?"

With a sigh she sat on her daughter's bed. *"Nee.* We talked about this. *Dat* will not come here again. He's gone to be with *Gott."*

"When I wake up?"

"Nee, not then either." Evelyn put a hand to her head. She was too tired to keep finding new ways to tell her daughter that her father was gone.

"Tell me a story, *Mamm?"*

"I'm too tired tonight. I'll tell you one tomorrow night."

"Water?"

Martha asked for water every time she was denied a story. It was a way to delay bedtime. Evelyn stood, and poured a glass of water from the pitcher and took it back to Martha. "You'll have to sit up."

Martha sat and placed both hands around the glass and took a small sip.

"Is that all?"

Martha giggled and nodded.

"You can't have been very thirsty."

Smiling, Martha slipped back under the covers.

"Gut nacht." Evelyn pulled the quilt back over Martha's shoulders, and then leaned down and kissed her forehead."

"Gut nacht," Martha's small voice replied.

Leaving the bedroom door slightly open, Evelyn headed downstairs.

Evelyn had underestimated the changes that would take place in her life after Amos' death. Small things that she'd taken for granted she'd either have to do herself or pay someone to do them. Once she was downstairs, she started a fire with the last of the chopped firewood. There was only half a basket of kindling and six large logs left. In the barn were enough logs of firewood to see her through the winter, but she'd have to learn to split them for herself. Being the youngest in the family meant that there was often no use her learning things. Splitting wood had been one of those chores that nobody had taken time to teach her. After she'd married, that had been one of Amos' chores. Evelyn was going to make sure she taught each of her children all she could. It takes time to teach a child skills, but, once taught, the child becomes a helper. It's a blessing in later life for the child to have learned such skills.

One of the many things in life she looked forward to was sitting alone and having a nice cup of hot tea in peace. She headed to the kitchen to boil the pot. Once the stove was lit, she picked up the kettle and filled it with water. On the way back to the stove, she noticed water dripping from somewhere. Looking closely at the kettle she saw that it was leaking. With a yell, she rushed back to the sink, but not before quite a bit of water had dripped onto the floor.

I'll put a new kettle on my list of things that'll never happen and things I'll never get. Nee! I need two separate lists—there'll be too many items for one list. Evelyn pulled a small saucepan out of the cupboard, filled it, and placed it on the stove. While waiting for it to boil, she filled the teapot with tea leaves and then placed a cup beside it.

"Are you all right, *Mamm?*" a small voice said behind her.

Evelyn jumped with fright and turned around to see Martha out of bed. "You'll catch your death of cold. Back to bed with you!"

"You screamed."

"I'm all right. It was just the kettle leaking." She looked down at the floor and realized she'd have to mop up the water. Looking back at Martha, she said, "I'll take you back to bed, and then you must stay there."

"Okay, *Mamm.*"

Evelyn took Martha back to bed and went through the same routine with her asking for a story, and then having a drink of water. Once Martha was settled for a second time, Evelyn headed back downstairs suddenly rushing when she remembered she had water on the stove. Before she reached the loudly bubbling water, she skidded on the wet floor and landed hard on her bottom.

Even though she was in pain, there was no time to waste. The water was now bubbling over and soon it would get into the gas connection. On her bottom, she scooted close to the oven and turned the stove off, but the flame died before she could reach it. She flicked the switch off. Not knowing much about the gas connection, she didn't know whether it was safe to use the oven again. If Amos had been alive, he would've known what to do with the oven.

It was a dreadful ending to a dreadful day. Evelyn pulled herself to her feet and rubbed her bottom, grateful that she'd landed on her behind rather than her front. She was certain her baby was unharmed.

Now covered in water and having dirtied her dress, she leaned over to see that there was scarcely any water left in the saucepan. Perhaps there was enough for half a cup? She poured the water into the teapot and swished it around. A few seconds later, she poured it into the cup through a strainer. There was barely half a cup of a strange-colored tea. She took her cup into the living room so she could warm herself in front of the fire.

Evelyn sat in her wet dress and drank the tea. If she'd gone upstairs and changed into her nightdress the tea would've grown cold and she liked her tea hot. She wondered whether it was worth the effort to boil water on the fire for some more tea, then considered the effort required would be too great.

Her bottom was still hurting from the hard fall but she had more urgent concerns than that. She'd try not to think about it today, but tomorrow she must figure out what to do about her sudden lack of finances. She now owned her home and her husband's old family home. Her own house was in need of repairs, but surely her late husband's family home would be able to be leased. Amos had claimed that he'd been doing repairs and Evelyn hoped what he'd said was true. Tomorrow she'd go there and find out exactly what state it was in.

She sat in her wet dress and looked around the living room. The paint was peeling off the top of the walls and there was a crack between two walls. She'd been watching it grow larger over the past year. The chimney hadn't been cleaned out for years—it was okay now, but given the choice Evelyn would've preferred to stop problems before they started. The last thing she wanted was a chimney fire like the Fishers' had last winter.

Even though she was trying her best to put things out of her mind until the next day, she could barely stop her mind from continuing to form the list of all the things that needed to be done. The most important thing was to get the gas stove working. She'd give it a day to dry out and try to light it again tomorrow. She took a third mouthful of tea, which was lukewarm. If she weren't so tired she could've put a pot on the fire to boil for a decent cup of hot tea. Normally she would've taken the cup back to the kitchen and washed it and put it away, but who cared about being tidy and clean right now? Certainly not Evelyn! After she placed the cup on the low table in the living room, she walked upstairs to change into her nightgown. Once she was changed she peeped into Martha's

SAMANTHA PRICE

room to see that she was sleeping soundly. Evelyn crept close to her bed and pulled the quilt over Martha's shoulder. *"Gut nacht,* my sweet *boppli."*

She walked down the staircase, stepping carefully on the bottom two steps that sorely needed attention, and headed back to the kitchen. One thing that would make her feel worse in the morning was seeing a mess. She grabbed the mop and cleaned the floor, leaving a dry track so she could fetch that cup from the living room. Once she'd done that and washed the cup, she mopped the rest of the kitchen floor.

Once the place was tidy, she checked to see how the fire was going. *One more log and it'll burn most of the night.* She picked up another log, careful to hold it in a way that she wouldn't get a splinter in her finger. From the log jumped a large spider. Evelyn threw the log, screamed and headed for the couch. Once she was on the couch, she drew her legs up under her. Her one big fear was spiders, and now there was one in her house. The worst thing was that she didn't see where it went. She was grateful that Martha was a sound sleeper—once she was asleep almost nothing would wake her.

"I can't go on like this, *Gott!"* It hit her that there was no Amos to locate the spider and no Amos to get the gas working again. There was no Amos to split more wood once the wood in the box ran out. Even though Evelyn had thought him useless when he'd been alive, now she was beginning to realize how hard things were going to be without him.

CHAPTER 3

This book of the law shall not depart out of thy mouth;
but thou shalt meditate therein day and night,
that thou mayest observe to do according to all
that is written therein:
for then thou shalt make thy way prosperous,
and then thou shalt have good success.
Joshua 1:8

EVELYN WOKE EARLY, and relit the fire before Martha woke. She made a cooking area in the fire, just like she'd seen in her *grossmammi's* house when she'd been a young girl. By the time she heard Martha's call, she'd already collected the eggs and had warm milk and porridge waiting. Most mornings Martha and Evelyn collected the eggs together.

After Evelyn had washed and dressed Martha, Martha sat at the low children's table to eat her breakfast.

"Dat coming today?"

"Nee!" Realizing she'd snapped at Martha, she leaned down close to her. *"Dat* is not ever coming back here because he doesn't live here anymore. *Dat* is gone—he's dead." Up until now, Evelyn had avoided using the word 'dead,' Evelyn hoped Martha might associate the dead animals she'd seen with the way her father was.

"Is he at *Grossdaddi's haus?"*

Evelyn stood up and sighed. Martha had never mentioned her father as much as she had over the past few days; she knew something was amiss where her father was concerned. *"Nee,* he's not there. He's with *Gott* and won't be coming back here to the *haus.* Now no more talk; eat up."

Walking over to the window, Evelyn's thoughts returned to the spider that had jumped at her the night before. She'd thought of little else that night while she was trying to sleep. Everything had felt like the spider was crawling on her—the prayer *kapp* strings as she was taking her *kapp* off—the edge of the sheet when she turned over—her hair when it brushed over her face during the night. It had been another sleepless night in a long string of them since Amos' death. Hopefully the spider had found its way outside, since there were enough cracks in the wall and spaces between the floorboards.

"Finish, *Mamm."*

"Already?" Evelyn turned to see Martha holding up her empty dish in one small hand. "Don't …" It was too late! The bowl had slipped out of Martha's hand and was on the floor in several pieces.

Martha looked at the mess on the floor and burst into tears.

"Don't cry; it was an accident. Stay there while I clean it up. Don't move."

Martha stayed in the chair while Evelyn fetched a bucket from outside the back door. As soon as she collected the pieces, she heard a buggy coming toward the house.

"We have visitors." Evelyn placed the bucket on the floor and held out her hand to Martha. Together they walked to the front door and opened it.

Martha had hoped it would be Sally or one of her other sisters; she wasn't so pleased when she saw it was Hezekiah.

"It's Mr. Hostetler," she said firmly to Martha hoping to prevent her daughter from calling him 'Dat.'

"Mister Hostetter," Martha repeated trying to say his name.

Holding firmly onto Martha's hand, Evelyn approached the buggy as soon as the horse came to a halt. "Hello," she said brightly trying to hide how she truly felt.

"Hello, Evelyn, and Martha."

"Hello, *Dat,*" Martha said in a small voice that could barely be heard.

"It's not *Dat,*" Evelyn hissed at her daughter before she looked up at Hezekiah hoping she wouldn't have to invite him inside the house. The only person who'd been in the house over the past years—besides her sisters and their families—was the midwife, Dana.

"It occurred to me that I should see if you have enough firewood. It was a cold night last night."

"Denke, that's so kind of you, but we're fine."

"You are?" He stared at her as if he knew she wasn't telling the truth.

She nodded. How could she tell him that she needed firewood chopped but didn't want to be indebted to anyone except maybe one of her brother-in-laws.

Then she noticed that he'd shaved his beard. She nearly choked. That meant he was looking for a wife, since all Amish men grow their beards when they get married. This was not good. The last thing she needed was a man who was far too old for her being interested in her.

"Is there anything else you need?"

Jah. She desperately wanted someone to go inside and find the spider to take it outside, but if she asked him in, he'd see the state of the house. If he saw how much there was to do around the house he might never leave. Evelyn giggled nervously. "You know how many *bruder*-in-laws I've got. They come and do things for me all the time—I mean, they have for the past few days since..."

"I see. I was passing by and I thought I should offer you my help." He looked down at Martha and ruffled her hair, which caused Martha to giggle. "I'd like to talk to you about something important, Evelyn, and I'm not certain it's for the ears of a child."

"Oh. I'll sit Martha on the couch and we can talk on the porch."

He nodded. In her heart, Evelyn hoped he wasn't going to propose. Since he'd shaved his beard off it was a possibility. After she placed Martha on the couch she gave her a doll to play with. "You sit there and be a *gut* girl. Mr. Hostetler and I are going to sit on the porch and talk."

"I come too."

"Nee. You sit there. We're having adults' talk. I can see

you from the porch so don't move off this couch or you'll get into trouble. I'll be back very soon."

"Okay, *Mamm.*"

Evelyn left her daughter in the living room and when she was on the porch, she looked through the window to make sure that Martha was still seated.

She sat on the seat next to Hezekiah.

"I'll get right to the heart of the matter. You and I have both lost our spouses so I thought we might join our households and *kinner* to become one *familye.*"

"You're asking me to marry you?"

"Jah. Do you think you could ever be interested in a man like me?"

She couldn't look at him. One loveless marriage in one lifetime had been enough, so why would she want another?

He added, "I know you might think it too soon to make such a decision, but I wanted to make it known that these are the feelings in my heart. It could save you problems in the future."

Problems in the future? I've enough of those in the present. Evelyn took a deep breath, then stood up to look through the window to make sure Martha had stayed put. She hadn't. Martha had climbed off the couch and was sitting on the floor. Evelyn knocked loudly on the window and when Martha looked up, Evelyn pointed at her; Martha promptly got back on the couch.

"I won't keep you. I'm sure you've got many things to do with looking after the little one and the next one coming along soon."

Evelyn felt her cheeks warm at the mention of her

pregnancy. It wasn't the usual thing to discuss pregnancy with men.

"I think you should consider my offer. Your life will be a lot easier if you have a husband. It's not good that a woman should be on her own with no man to take care of her."

From the past few days she'd had, Evelyn knew that what he said was true. How good it would be to have a man to care for her, but why couldn't it be a man her heart desired? Rather than tell him it was out of the question, and tell him all the reasons why, she said, "It's far too soon to even consider such a thing."

"Soon it won't be easy for you on your own."

Soon? It's already too hard on my own. She nodded and looked down. "Where are your *kinner* today?"

"My *schweschder* minds them while I'm working; I'm on my way there now." He stood. *"Denke* for hearing what I had to say."

"Denke for asking."

"The offer is there, Evelyn."

She stood up too, and after a quick glance through the window at her daughter, she nodded to him.

"Even if you don't accept my offer, I'm happy to help out where and when needed."

"Denke." She appreciated his offer, but would not take him up on it.

Relief swept through her when Hezekiah left her house.

When she walked inside she heard her daughter say, "Has *Dat* gone?"

Not knowing whether she meant Hezekiah or her real

father, she nodded, too weary to want to know. *"Dat* has gone. Now, we're going to visit *Grossdaddi's haus."*

"See *grossdaddi?"*

"Nee." It was no use: it was back to explaining. *"Grossdaddi* and *Dat* have gone to be with *Gott* and they're not coming back. They're both living in *Gott's haus* now." Amos' father had died only six months before he had.

Her daughter's eyes grew wider.

"We're going to see how the *haus* looks, and hopefully, it will be in gut order so we can lease it out. If we can, then we'll have money to buy food. Otherwise, we'll have no money for food." Evelyn knew Martha was too young to fully understand what she was saying.

"Okay, *Mamm."*

Her late father-in-law's house was walking distance away, but too far to walk with a small child.

She loaded Martha in the back of the buggy and led the horse out of the stall. Glancing down at the dirty stall, she knew that later that day she'd have to clean it out—another job that Amos wasn't there to do anymore. It was tiring for a woman in her condition to hitch the buggy, but it was a job that had to be done unless she wanted to remain at home or be dependent upon others.

Once she pulled up outside the old house, she got Martha out and held her hand. She stared at the house pleased that it was clean and tidy on the outside. There wasn't a garden, but the lawn was weed-free and looked well cared for apart from needing mowing.

"Let's have a look inside, Martha."

"Okay, *Mamm."*

After Evelyn located the key that had been placed under a mat on the porch, she unlocked the door. A stale-damp smell immediately met her nostrils. "We need to open some windows. This smells horrible."

Before she took two steps into the house it was evident that it was in even worse repair than the one she lived in. A quick glance at the ceiling located the source of the stench. There were dark mold-filled drip marks down the walls. The roof was leaking.

Next, she stepped into the kitchen to see that there was a small wood-burning stove and many of the cupboard doors were missing. "How did your *vadder* live like this?" she murmured to Martha without thinking. Amos couldn't have been doing work to the *haus* unless he was doing it upstairs where the bedrooms were.

"Let's have a look upstairs." She took a firm hold of Martha's hand and headed to the staircase. When the first step felt as though it would collapse underfoot, she decided against going up the stairs.

She took another look around. "What happened to all the furniture?" she asked out loud. Her daughter stared up at her. There was only one chair and nothing else in the living room, and only two chairs to the dining room table. "I won't even try sitting in one of those chairs. Looks like I'll need to sell your *vadder's* buggy horse."

Mark was keeping Amos' buggy and horse at his property.

"Let's go and visit *Onkel* Mark and Aunt Sally."

"Jah!" Martha was always pleased to visit so she could play with Daniel and David.

CHAPTER 4

Commit thy works unto the Lord,
and thy thoughts shall be established.
Proverbs 16:3

WHEN SHE PULLED up at her sister's place a little further along the same road, she saw Mark with another man in a distant paddock.

Sally came out of the house to greet her. As soon as Martha was lifted out of the buggy, she asked Sally where the boys, her cousins, were. Martha wasn't too happy to hear they were in school.

Evelyn and Martha walked with Sally back into the house.

"I've just been over to look at William's old *haus.*"

"You shouldn't keep calling it William's house, it's yours now."

"I know, but in my mind it's still my *vadder*-in-law's *haus*."

"Anyway, what was the state of it?"

"Like I thought—dreadful. I told you I thought it would be."

Sally shook her head. "Come into the kitchen and I'll make you a nice cup of tea."

Making tea reminded Evelyn about her stove that wasn't working. Maybe it would work later today once the water dried out. She was reluctant to mention that things needed to be done around her house.

Sally leaned down to talk to Martha. "Why don't I gather you some toys to play with while your *mamm* and I talk?"

Martha nodded.

Sally spread out a blanket on the floor of the kitchen, and placed toys on top. "There you are, Martha, you can sit there and play until they come home."

"Denke," Martha said as she sat on the blanket.

A noise at the doorway of the house prompted Sally to say, "I forgot to tell you we've got a visitor."

Evelyn recalled the man she'd just seen in the fields with Mark, but before any more could be said, two men stood at the kitchen door. Evelyn turned to see Mark and a tall stranger. He was a handsome man with strong broad shoulders, tan skin, blue eyes and dusty blonde hair. Evelyn's eyes locked onto his, causing her tummy to flutter.

Martha ran to Mark and wrapped her arms around his leg.

"Hello, Martha," Mark said.

"Play with me?"

He laughed. "I might have time to play with you later. I've got work to do and I've got a friend visiting. This is Mr. Esh."

"Hello, Mr. Esh."

"It's nice to meet you, Martha."

She gave a little giggle.

"Look at all those toys, are they yours?" the stranger asked Martha.

"Nee; the cousins' toys."

"You go back and play now and then we can go outside later, okay?" Her Uncle Mark suggested.

"Okay." Martha ran back to the blanket.

Immediately Evelyn felt drawn to this man who had spoken so kindly to her daughter.

"Evelyn King, this is Jebediah Esh."

The stranger laughed. "Please—just Jed."

"Hello, Jed," Evelyn said, not being able to stop the smile that pulled at her lips.

"I heard about the funeral yesterday, and about your…"

Mark dug Jed in the ribs and nodded at young Martha, letting him know not to say too much in front of her. Mark continued, "Jed's staying with us for a few weeks looking for work."

"That's partly true. I do like to move around and see different parts of the country."

"Where are you from?" Evelyn asked.

"Ohio." His eyes fell to her stomach and then he drew his eyes away.

"Jed is traveling, doing jobs so he can save to buy a house for his new wife."

"I can speak for myself, Mark," Jed said with a laugh.

"You're newly married, Jed?" Evelyn asked.

"Nee, but I will be soon." He stared at Evelyn so intently she had to wonder what he thought of her.

Martha stood and tugged Mark's trouser leg. "We have no money for food, and Mister Hoster is not *Dat,"* Martha said in a voice too clear for her age.

"Martha! That's not so—I mean, the part about no money! The part about Mr. Hostetler not being your *vadder* is true." Evelyn said, wondering when she'd uttered words about having no money in front of her daughter. She must've, otherwise where would Martha have gotten it from? Evelyn shook her head. "I don't know where she gets these things from that come out of her mouth."

Martha stared at her mother and remained silent.

Sally laughed to cover up the awkward moment. "Go back and play, Martha. It's time for adults to talk." When Martha obeyed, Sally said, "Evelyn was just telling me she needs someone to fix her late *vadder*-in-law's *haus."*

Evelyn stared at her sister open-mouthed. What she'd told her wasn't meant to be repeated.

"Really? What needs doing?" Jed asked.

Evelyn shook her head. "Oh nothing. It's all right."

Mark said, "Why don't we go and have a look together? You need to get the place fixed so you can lease it, don't you?"

Evelyn looked over at Sally—she must've told him that.

"Go on," Sally said. "Why don't you go there now—the three of you, and I'll mind Martha."

"That sounds like a *gut* idea," Mark said. "It's not far."

"I suppose so." Evelyn figured maybe God had provided someone who could fix the house, and if so, God would also find a way to pay for it. Sure, the community would've rallied around and fixed the house, but Evelyn didn't want them to do that. "We can go in my buggy," she suggested.

The three of them walked into the house and Mark went straight to the mold. He pointed to the dark stains high on the walls. "This is black mold and that's toxic."

"You mean it's poisonous?"

"*Jah;* it's horrendous. It can make people really ill, particularly if they have an allergy to it. Even if they're not allergic, it can cause fatigue, memory problems, and depression. Has anyone been living here?"

"Not for some time." She couldn't say her late husband preferred living in this run-down house rather than to live with his family. "My *vadder*-in-law died a few months ago."

"I'll have to get up and have a look at the roof. Do you know if there's a ladder in the barn?" Jed asked.

"I'm not sure."

"I'll go and have a look," Mark said.

"While he's gone, I'll have a look upstairs and have a look in the loft space for signs of water damage."

"Mind the stairs. Some of them look dangerous."

He put his foot on the first step and avoided it, stepping on the second step. He was gone for several minutes before he joined her again. "Are you certain someone hasn't been living here? There is paperwork, and men's clothing and things are out, as though someone's been staying here." He gave Evelyn a look and she wondered if he'd found something in the bedroom that spoke of her late husband's living arrangements.

"My husband stayed here a couple of times. He was

about to start work on the place. He probably left things here." It was partly true since Amos had said he was working on the house.

"That explains it, then. I was afraid you might have a trespasser living here."

"Nee, I'm certain I don't."

He looked around with his hands on his hips. "I suppose no one would want to live here in these conditions."

Mark stuck his head in the door. "Okay. I've got a ladder ready. I'd go up there myself, but you'd know better what needs fixing."

"Convenient for you." Jed laughed before he headed out the door.

Evelyn put a hand to her throbbing head. She knew she had to be aware of what needed fixing, but at the same time it was a burden that weighed heavily.

She followed Mark outside and stood next to him while they watched Jed on the roof.

"How long have you known Jed?" she asked Mark.

"I've known him for most of my life. We went to *schul* together."

"I suppose you know that I'm not in a good place financially. I've got Amos' buggy horse I can sell, but I don't know if that'll be enough money to cover everything."

"Don't concern yourself, Evelyn. I'll make certain that the men come and fix things for you. And anything else you need, Sally and I will be happy to help."

"Nee, I couldn't even ask that." She knew that Sally and Mark were only just getting by themselves—helping her out would be an unfair burden on them.

"Leave it to me."

"Nee! I'll find out how much it costs first and whether I can afford to get it done. I might have to sell it just as it is."

"Don't worry. Jed can do electrical, plumbing, roofs and just about anything."

She glanced up at the roof to see Jed was now looking down at them.

CHAPTER 5

And thou shalt love the Lord thy God with all thine heart,
and with all thy soul, and with all thy might.
Deuteronomy 6:5

"WELL, HOW'S IT LOOKING?" Mark yelled to Jed still on the roof.

"Not too bad. I can see where the water's coming in. It just needs some flashing replaced; everything else looks good. The tiles that meet the chimney are often the weak point on the roof, but these look fine."

Evelyn breathed out a sigh of relief. That would save her ten to fifteen thousand dollars, which was what she'd guessed a new roof would've cost.

"The gutters need cleaning out; things are growing in them." He pulled out a tall weed and threw it down. "I won't know if they're going to need replacing until they're cleaned." He looked at Evelyn. "They'll be overflowing when it rains, and water will be getting into the ceiling and seeping down the walls. What I'll have to do is clean them out and then run water along the gutters to see if there are leaks."

"Okay," Evelyn agreed.

Mark looked at her. "All *gut* so far."

"It'll only be *gut* if they don't leak." She guessed that brand-new gutters all the way around the house would cost at least two thousand dollars and maybe more.

Jed laughed. "I'll take a closer look on the other side."

When Jed was out of view, Evelyn whispered to Mark, "His fiancée must be happy to have a man who's so handy. He could build his own *haus* by the sound of things." Why did *Gott* give things to some people and not to others? She would've been happy with a man like Jed.

Mark whispered back, "I guess she's happy. He hasn't told me much about her."

Jed appeared and climbed down the ladder. "It all looks not too bad. I'll make a list of things that need to be done about the place."

"Would you? That would be *wunderbaar.*"

"Do you have pen and paper?" He smiled at her as he dusted dirt from his hands against his thighs.

"I'm certain I have—in the buggy." She turned, and hurried to find pen and paper. When she climbed into the buggy, she looked back at Jed who was now talking with Mark. Evelyn could picture her now—the blessed woman that was to marry him. She'd be humble, and well mannered with a small polite giggle when someone said something funny. Of course, she'd be fair-haired and blue-eyed as Jed was, she'd have a pale flawless complexion. Her mind went on to picture Jed standing in front of his fiancée—her head would only reach his chin so he'd have to bend down to kiss her. Suddenly, he looked in her direction and she drew her eyes away from him, her gaze landing on a pen and a notebook on the floor of the buggy. She grabbed them both and headed back to him.

"*Denke,* Evelyn." He smiled at her.

Her body tingled at the sound of her name on his lips. She was certain that he felt something for her too, but why would he? It didn't make sense for him to feel anything for a woman who'd been recently widowed, a pregnant woman, and especially one with an outspoken three-year-old daughter. But still, it made her feel good to imagine that he had the same thoughts toward her.

Evelyn was pleased. For the first time, finally, she was attracted to a man. Her feelings meant that it might be possible for her to find love in the future. The butterflies in her tummy were what she'd been missing with Amos, proving that the old ladies had been wrong—she shouldn't have married Amos. Even though love was more than butterflies, surely it had to start with that feeling in one's tummy? She should've waited for love to come her way rather than accepting Amos' marriage proposal. If she'd waited, she might have met Jed before he proposed to his fiancée and who knows what would've happened?

"Let's go back inside, Evelyn."

Evelyn walked back into the house with Jed beside her.

He looked up at the mold. "*Nee,* on second thought, you shouldn't be in here until that's gone. You wait outside, and I'll make the list on my own. It's too dangerous for you to be here with the mold."

Evelyn walked outside and waited with Mark who'd

just put the ladder back in the barn. "It seems there are many things that need fixing." At once, Evelyn grew annoyed at her late husband. He'd led her to believe he was staying at the house to fix it, but what had been done?

"We'll see that it gets fixed. Don't look so worried," Mark said.

"I am worried." She nibbled on a fingernail. "I can't sell or lease this *haus* in the state it's in."

"Which will you do?"

"I want to have someone live here, leasing it." She didn't want to tell Mark that she needed the money to live on. He wouldn't have any idea that Amos had died a poor man. Even though they had two houses, the money from his job only lasted from week to week.

"The *gut* thing is, it doesn't need a new roof."

"Jah, that was a piece of *gut* news." Evelyn knew she had to be grateful for that.

Half an hour later, Jed came out of the *haus* with the list in his hand. "Shall we go back to your place, Mark, so I can run though the list with Evelyn?"

"Perhaps we should. It looks like you've listed quite a few things."

"Some are urgent, others aren't so pressing," Jed said. "It is imperative to get to the mold and find the cause of it, which will be the flashing on the roof and the gutters, I'd say. We need to fix that first and kill the mold."

"Denke, Jed, when I know exactly what's wrong I'll work on my budget and figure out what to do first."

"Why don't Mark and I organize some men to come here and fix everything? If we have enough people we could get it all done in a matter of days."

Evelyn put her fingertips to her forehead. *"Nee.* I must

think things through. *Denke* for what you've done so far." She licked her lips. "How long are you staying on here, Jed?"

"I'm not certain of that. If you want me to help with the *haus*, I'll stay until it's finished." He smiled. "You don't need to worry about that. I won't be running off anywhere."

She managed to smile back. Running off was what she was used to Amos doing.

Once they were back at Mark and Sally's house, Jed ran through the list of repairs. He ended up talking about the kitchen cabinets. "They don't need to be done immediately, but they were only made out of plywood and they've been water damaged. That's why there are some doors missing. They most likely disintegrated."

"Sounds like they need doing right away. I can't have someone come in to lease the *haus* with no cupboard doors in the kitchen."

"What I mean by not being urgent is that it's not a structural problem, whereas most of the other items on the list are."

Evelyn ran her eyes down the long list. "I see what you mean."

Sally came into the kitchen holding Martha's hand.

"Play with me now?" Martha asked Jed.

Jed laughed and then looked at Evelyn. "I did say I'd play with her."

Evelyn nodded.

Jed turned back to Martha. "Shall we find *Onkel* Mark and see if he wants to play hide and seek with us?"

Martha squealed with excitement and bounced up and down on the balls of her feet.

Jed took hold of her hand and while they walked out of the kitchen, Sally sat down at the table. "Handsome and *gut* with children."

"Sh, Sally."

"He can't hear me. He's out of the *haus* by now."

"Well, it won't do me any good. He's already getting married to someone else."

"*Jah*, it's a shame you didn't meet him sooner."

"It wouldn't have done any good because I was married to Amos."

Sally nodded. "That's true. I'm sorry."

Evelyn grunted. "You don't have to be sorry. You know what my marriage to Amos was like."

"That's what I'm sorry about."

"Oh. I forgot to tell you. Hezekiah Hostetler asked me to marry him."

"*Nee!*" As Sally giggled, someone cleared his throat in the doorway of the kitchen. Evelyn turned to see Jed standing there.

"Excuse me for interrupting, but Martha is asking if she'll still be here when the boys get home from *schul.*"

Evelyn's heart froze. He'd overheard! Now he'd think of her as a gossiping woman to reveal a thing as private as a marriage proposal. She smiled brightly to cover her embarrassment. "*Jah*. We'll stay so she can play with them for a little while."

"I'll let her know. She'll be pleased about that. And—congratulations on that proposal." He gave her a wink before he disappeared.

CHAPTER 6

Let no corrupt communication proceed out of your mouth,
but that which is good to the use of edifying,
that it may minister grace unto the hearers.
Ephesians 4:29

EVELYN COVERED her mouth and looked at Sally.

"Don't worry. He won't repeat it."

"Ach nee. I didn't mean for him to hear it." She wasn't worried about him telling someone so much—it was what he would think of her that mattered. What if he thought that she liked Hezekiah and was going to accept the proposal? That would seem quite reasonable to Jed because he didn't even know who Hezekiah was.

"What did you say to Hezekiah? You were just about to tell me."

Evelyn sighed and looked at Sally. "I'm not going to

marry him, of course. Why would I? He's years older than I am."

"I know that, silly, but what did you say to let him down gently? I know he's far too old for you and totally unsuited."

"I said it was too soon after Amos died."

"That was clever thinking." Sally leaned over and patted her on the hand. *"Jah,* good thinking, that was the best thing to say."

"Then he asked if I had anything that needed doing around the house."

"That was nice of him. You'd have things for him to do, wouldn't you?"

"Sally! I couldn't have him do anything. I'd feel obligated and it wouldn't be right."

"I know, I was just joking—trying to be funny, but he *did* ask."

Evelyn stared at her sister. She seemed blissfully unaware of the complexities of Evelyn's life as it was. If only Jed hadn't heard that someone had asked her to marry him. But then again, he was getting married himself so what did it matter? "So, your new houseguest is getting married soon?"

"He is, and I don't know why it's taken so long for him. He's very handsome, don't you think?"

"Of course, he is. I'd have to agree. He's one of the nicest looking men I've seen. And it'd be handy to marry a builder—someone who could fix things." That's what Evelyn needed more than anything right now; a man who could fix things, repair houses and chop wood. If she'd had a man right now he could've started with the gas stove.

Sally leaned over. "Too late! He's already getting married; he's found a *fraa.*"

Evelyn laughed. "Keep reminding me and I'll hit you with something."

Sally laughed.

"It is nice to know there are men like that around." Evelyn stood up and looked out the kitchen window. "Sally, come and see how he's playing with Martha. He's completely won her over in such a short time."

Sally stood beside her and peered out the window. A giggle escaped her lips as she watched Jed spinning Martha around in a circle.

"Amos never ever played with her like that. I often wondered whether it was because he wanted a boy."

"Did he want a boy?"

Evelyn shrugged her shoulders. "He never said so."

"Don't be so hard on Amos. He was probably too busy working hard to provide for both of you."

Evelyn couldn't help feeling a little betrayed by Sally's comment. She'd shared with Sally how her marriage had been, and now Sally was defending Amos. "I didn't mean to speak badly of him, it's just that—I was saying how it was. I would've wanted a husband to take more interest in his *kinner* than Amos did. It was as though he was going through everything in life that he was supposed to do rather than enjoying the moments."

Sally scrunched up her nose. "What do you mean?"

With her shoulders now rounded she searched for words to express her feelings. "He had to get married, so he married me, then the next step was *kinner,* so we had a *boppli.* Amos seemed to be doing things because they were expected of him rather than doing them because he wanted to do them. If you ask me, he didn't want to be a *vadder* at all—much less, a husband."

Sally nodded then looked out the window again. "It must've been hard for you with him spending so much time away."

"He found something displeasing about me, but I don't know what."

Sally lunged for her arm and held it. Looking into Evelyn's eyes, she said, "The fault must've been with him. There's nothing wrong with you. He should've been pleased to have you as his *fraa*."

"*Denke,* Sally, but how would you know what a man likes?"

"Don't doubt yourself. *Menner* don't need much to keep them satisfied, believe me, and I'm certain you did everything to make him happy."

"That's true; I did." She stared back out the window at Jed and her daughter. Martha was now chasing Jed as he swerved and circled just out of her reach. Mark sat not far from them looking on. Hearing Martha's giggles filled Evelyn with happiness. "All I wanted was for Amos to want to be with us, and for him to want to play with Martha just like that."

Sally rubbed her arm. "You remember what *Mamm* used to say?"

"About regrets?"

Sally nodded.

"A waste of time," Evelyn stated just as their mother would've said it.

"That's right. And that's true. You weren't to know that Amos would be like he was. You married him in faith that he would be a *gut* husband and a *gut vadder*."

A tear trickled down Evelyn's cheek before she wiped it away with the back of her hand. "Sometimes I feel that *Gott* let me down. Look how happy you and Mark are. Amos and I were never happy like that."

Sally slowly nodded and remained silent. Even though she had no answer or comment, Evelyn felt comforted that she'd acknowledged her pain.

She looked out at Jed again to see that Sally's boys had joined Jed and Martha. "The boys are home."

"Cake and cookie time," Sally said as she moved away from the window.

Evelyn stepped back when Jed glanced in the direction of the kitchen window. After a few seconds, she peeped out once more. When she noticed he was now playing with the boys as well, she kept studying him. How happy would she be if she'd married someone like him; someone bright and cheerful who took an interest in his *kinner* and didn't feel the need to be on his own?

"Stop staring," Sally hissed.

Evelyn giggled. "Okay, but it's not easy."

"Sit down and I'll cut you a piece of cake. Give that *boppli* of yours some food."

Evelyn put a hand on her stomach, over her baby, and then sat down at the kitchen table. *"Denke,* and then Martha and I will have to go home. We've got a few things to do before it gets dark." Besides the dinner to prepare, there was the horse's stall to clean, the horse and the chickens had to be fed, and their water needed to be changed. She hoped that the stove would be working by the time she got home or she'd have to cook over the fire once more. *The fire—ach!* She desperately needed wood chopped.

CHAPTER 7

God is not a man, that he should lie; neither the son of man, that he should repent: hath he said, and shall he not do it? or hath he spoken, and shall he not make it good?
Numbers 23:19

WHEN SHE AND Martha were leaving Sally's house, Jed was near her buggy.

"Goodbye, Martha. Bye, Evelyn."

"Bye, Jed," Evelyn said wondering why he was now walking toward them.

"Need a hand?" he asked.

"Nee, we're fine. About what you overheard just now…"

He raised his eyebrows and his eyes locked onto hers. "Your proposal of marriage?"

"Jah. I'm not going to accept—he's a lovely man and would make someone a gut husband, but not me."

He nodded and kept staring, which made her feel like she had to explain further. "Besides that, my husband has only just died. There should be a suitable time that passes before I'd ever consider a thing like that."

He folded his arms and leaned back.

"And Hezekiah's older, a lot older—you'll see that if you stay around long enough to meet him. I wasn't making fun of him or gossiping about him. Well, I suppose I was talking about him, which might be the same, although I wasn't being cruel."

Finally, he spoke. "I'm glad you pointed that out."

"I thought I should. I didn't want you to get the wrong idea." Evelyn rubbed her neck. She wanted to scratch— certain that her nerve rash was coming back. "I just wanted you to know that I'm not *that* kind of person."

He nodded his head once, sharply. *"Gut!"*

"You could lift Martha into the buggy for me."

"I'd be glad to." He reached down and placed Martha in the buggy.

"Denke," Martha said in a small voice.

"You're welcome, Martha. *Denke* for allowing me to play with you today."

Martha giggled.

"Goodbye, Jed." Evelyn was now in the driver's seat.

Jed stepped back from the buggy. "Farewell," he said with a bow.

She turned the buggy around and headed away from him, convinced she shouldn't have said anything at all. Her mother had always told her that men didn't like women who talked too much. Perhaps that was her problem she thought as her horse clip-clopped down the long driveway.

44

Amos had bought the house she was currently living in with money his father had gotten when he sold off most of his farmland. Amos had been an only child. Perhaps Amos was so used to being alone, he didn't know how to share his life with others.

The two houses were, she hoped, debt free, but from what she'd recently found out about Amos and his dealings, she'd have to pay a visit to the local land titles office to see if it was owned free and clear. *Maybe that's the answer—I could borrow against one of the houses.* She shook her head and groaned when she realized she'd have no way to pay back a loan.

Once she got home there were many outside chores to be done with the animals. When they were done she walked inside and looked down at the wood box. There was only enough wood until tomorrow. She waited until it was very cold before she lit the fire hoping to save as much wood as she could.

Perhaps, she thought, *Gott* is testing me and allowing me only what I need to get through each day—one day at a time. Evelyn recalled a story from the Bible, in 1 Kings 17, about the jar of flour that never ran out and the oil that never ran dry—just as the Lord had promised to Elijah.

She picked up the large black Bible that Amos had read out of when he'd been home. Flicking through the pages, she found it and read the passage aloud "And the barrel of meal wasted not, neither did the cruse of oil fail, according to the word of the Lord, which he spake by Elijah."

Needing some encouragement that God was still with her, she read the previous few pages. *She was a widow too!*

She read how Elijah had met a widow in a great famine and asked the widow for food. The widow told him they had barely any food for herself and her son. She'd intended to prepare their last meal and then they would die. Elijah told the widow to carry on as planned, but first to make a loaf of bread for him before she made loaves for herself and her son. If she did as instructed, he assured her the oil and flour would never run out until rain fell on the land once more.

She closed the Bible. God was telling her she had to find ways to be more giving. Even though she had barely anything to give, perhaps she could give of her time. *If Gott is telling me to do that then that is exactly what I must do.* Shutting her eyes, she asked God to bring her someone she could help, or to show her how she could be of service to someone.

Feeling at peace, she turned off the overhead gaslight, and climbed the stairs with a kerosene lamp in hand to light her way.

CHAPTER 8

But my God shall supply all your need
according to his riches in glory by Christ Jesus.
Philippians 4:19

EVELYN WOKE the next morning pleased to wake before
Martha. The older Martha got, the longer she was sleep-
ing-in of a morning, and that suited Evelyn just fine. As
much as she was devoted to Martha, she cherished quiet
moments alone as she watched the sun rise. Today,
though, it was too cold to get out of bed. She pulled the
quilt higher over her head, so she could breathe in the
warm air. Her baby was going to be a winter baby and
that would make more work.

Evelyn closed her eyes tighter and tried to avoid
making another mental list of all that needed to be done
before the baby arrived. The stove still wasn't working
and the night before, after cleaning out the stable and

doing the other chores, Evelyn had only enough energy to cook a meal. Now the pot and the plates she'd used for that meal were lying in the sink waiting to be washed.

She sighed and wished she'd made the effort last night. Her standards couldn't slip just because she was tired. If she got used to seeing the house a mess, a mess it might stay. Waking up to a tidy kitchen had always made her feel good, and knowing those dishes awaited her was another reason to stay in bed that much longer.

The next thing Evelyn knew was that a small hand was on her shoulder shaking her.

"*Mamm,* wake up. *Dat's* here."

Evelyn rubbed her eyes and could tell by the light filtering through the window that she'd slept way past the ten minutes she had intended. She looked at her shivering daughter.

"Come on, we better get you changed into some warm clothes."

"*Dat's* here."

"*Nee* he's not here. He won't be back, he's with *Gott* now."

"He's here," Martha insisted.

"Mr. Hostetler's downstairs; is that what you mean?

Martha nodded.

Evelyn sighed. "You get into my bed and stay warm. I'll be back as soon as I go and see what he wants." Evelyn stripped off her nightgown, pulled on her dress and over-apron, and then pushed her hair under her prayer *kapp.* She looked down at her bare feet and pulled on black stockings. "Stay there," she said firmly to Martha.

Evelyn reminded herself not to hurry down the stairs.

"Hezekiah!" she said as she opened the door. "I didn't

hear you knocking." By the position of the sun in the sky, Evelyn guessed it to be around nine or ten in the morning.

"Martha answered the door. I hope I didn't give her a fright. She still seems to think I'm her *vadder*," he said with a grin.

"Did she call you that again?"

He laughed. "She did. I'm here because I heard you're getting some work done at William's old *haus*."

"That's right. I had Mark and a friend of his take a look at it yesterday."

"I'm quite happy to help."

She looked down her stockinged feet and then back up to his face. "I do appreciate your offer. There are so many things happening at once I can't quite keep track of them. Mark is looking after things and he said he might ask for help from the community."

"There is something else I wanted to talk to you about. Something regarding Amos, but I don't know if now is the right time."

"What is it about?"

"It's about Amos and money."

Amos and money were two things that didn't go together in her mind, so she had no idea what he was about to say."

"You must tell me, Hezekiah."

"It's not an easy thing for me to say."

Normally she would've asked him into the kitchen but she didn't want anyone to see the disrepair the place was in.

"Then we'll sit here on the porch and you can tell me."

After they were seated, Hezekiah took a deep breath and said, "Amos borrowed money from me."

Evelyn gasped. "He did?"

Hezekiah nodded. *"Jah,* he did. I wasn't sure if you knew about it, but then it seemed you didn't. You would've mentioned it to me if you had."

"Jah, of course, I would've. How much did he borrow?" Evelyn took a deep breath. Any amount would've been too much. Amos had never even hinted at the fact that he'd borrowed money from anyone.

"A sizeable sum. He needed it because he'd been laid off his job a year ago."

"Nee, that's not right; he was working."

Hezekiah shook his head. "The business he was working for closed down six months ago and they laid most of their workers off a year ago. Amos was amongst the first of the employees to be let go."

She put a hand to her churning stomach. Why had he never told her he'd lost his job?

"He told me his situation and asked me for money. At first it was a little money, but he was back the first of every month to borrow more." Hezekiah shrugged his shoulders. "I had the money to give so I gave it to him."

"How much was it?"

"Altogether it was $42,300."

Evelyn shook her head. "That can't be right."

Just when God was telling her she had to be more giving, it seemed He was testing her further. Now she was sinking further into debt and needing even more money.

"I have all the paperwork. He signed every time I gave him money. It started out with five hundred dollars and then the next time it was more."

"Forgive me, Hezekiah, I'm not doubting your words, or the fact that you gave him money. I'm surprised, that's all. He never mentioned any of it to me." At the realization that she would have to pay the money back, tears trickled down her cheeks. She wiped them away the best she could.

"I don't need the money; that's not why I'm here. When you didn't mention it when we last spoke, I guessed you knew nothing about it—your financial situation."

"I'll pay you back; every cent of it."

He sucked in his cheeks. "I don't want to cause you concern. Just make payments a little bit at a time—whatever you can manage when you can manage it."

"I'll make sure I do." She tried to be bright to cover up how upset she was.

"I noticed when I was talking to Martha at the door, there is nothing left in your wood box."

Everlyn nodded. "That's right, I have to split more wood today. There's plenty in the wood shed."

"I'll do that for you. I don't have to be anywhere today until midday."

She shook her head. "I can't have you do that."

"And I can't not do that for a woman in your condition." He gave a chuckle. "It's not a hard thing for me to do."

With more tears threatening, all Evelyn could do was nod in agreement. He was such a kind and generous man, and the only man who'd gone out of his way to ask if she needed help—apart from her *bruder*-in-laws.

"I didn't tell you about your husband's loan to upset you."

"I know you wouldn't do that. It was just such a shock

51

that he didn't tell me about his job, and that he left us in debt."

"He would've planned to get a job, pay me back and hope you'd never know. It would've been a dreadful thing for Amos to not have been able to provide for you and Martha."

Evelyn nodded, not entirely agreeing. Amos had not been the man most people thought him to be.

Hezekiah sprang to his feet. "I'll get to work then."

As he walked to the woodshed near the house, Evelyn remembered Martha was still in her bed. When she walked into the house, she saw Martha sitting on the wooden stairs in her cotton nightdress. "Martha! I told you stay in my bed where it's warm."

"I want to see Mr. Hofstetter."

"You can see him again when he's finished chopping the wood. Now let's get into some clothes and then we'll get you some breakfast."

While Evelyn warmed up Martha's oatmeal over the fire, she raced in to inspect the kitchen in case Hezekiah happened to go in there. She saw the dishes from the night before, and quickly filled them with water and soap. She wiped down everything else with a damp rag. *That looks much better!*

She hurried back to the oatmeal just as it was bubbling in the pot. Then she spooned the oatmeal into two bowls. She sat at the kitchen table eating oatmeal with Martha, to the sound of log splitting. The noise had never sounded so good. With every chopping sound, she was reminded that it was one less job she'd have to do.

Now that she had some quiet time, her thoughts traveled to Amos' debt, which had now become hers. Why didn't he tell her he'd lost his job? And more importantly, why hadn't anyone else in the community mentioned it? Besides Hezekiah, someone else in their tight-knit community must have known.

The amount Amos borrowed added up to be over a year of his wages. But now she wasn't so sure what he had earned. Maybe nothing he'd told her was true.

It was good of Hezekiah to say that she could pay it back in bits and pieces, but she had no idea where she could get money. She added up her assets, which were the two houses, the two buggies and the two buggy horses. The good buggy had to be kept; one buggy horse and the old buggy could be sold. Then she could figure out what to do with the houses. The worst thing she thought of would be that she'd have to sell everything and go to live with one of her sisters.

She might have to speak to the bishop; perhaps he would figure out a way she could get money or have the community help with the house. Evelyn bit her lip when she realized that Mark was looking after all that.

CHAPTER 9

Therefore I say unto you, What things soever ye desire,
when ye pray, believe that ye receive them,
and ye shall have them.
Mark 11:24

WHEN EVELYN REALIZED that the sounds of the wood chopping had stopped, she hurried to the door to see Hezekiah walking toward her dusting off his hands.

"Come inside and wash up."

"Denke."

After he walked through the door, she asked, "Would you like tea or *kaffe?*"

"Kaffe please."

"Coming right up. The bathroom is just past the stairs." She pointed to the bathroom and then she went back to the kitchen silently praying that the stove would work. She flicked the switch to 'on' and was pleased to hear the sound of gas. After striking a match she held it to the hotplate, and watched as the flame burned brightly. *Denke Gott.*

After she got everything prepared for the coffee the only thing left to do was wait for the pot to boil. She spun around when she heard Hezekiah's footsteps at the doorway of the kitchen. "That was quick. Have a seat."

When he sat, she sat down across from him.

"*Denke* for splitting the wood. I was going to ask Mark, but didn't like to mention it because he's so busy."

He smiled. "Before I go I'll fill the wood box for you."

She smiled back. "That would be *gut.* You mentioned William's *haus.* I thought that if I get it fixed, I could lease it out." Normally she would never discuss financial matters with anyone, but now that she'd learned she owed him money, he needed to know what her circumstances were. She nervously fidgeted with her fingernails.

"That'll be the pot boiling."

"Oh! I didn't hear it." She fixed him a coffee and placed it in front of him. "Do you have milk or sugar?"

He shook his head. "I take it black."

She made a cup of tea for herself and sat down again. All the while, Martha had been sitting quietly at her own small table looking from one to the other. Now, she banged her spoon on her bowl.

"Stop that, Martha. Do you want more?"

"*Jah!*"

"Well, you must ask nicely."

"More please."

"All right." Evelyn took her bowl and filled it up from the pot that was now on the sink. "There you are," she said as she placed the bowl down.

She looked over at Hezekiah to see him staring at her. Evelyn regretted asking him in for coffee, but what could she do after he had split so much wood for her? "I appreciate all the chopping of the wood you've done for me today."

He smiled. "It wasn't much for me to do. Is there anything else you need me to do while I'm here?"

"Nee." She shook her head. "I can't think of anything at all. I did have a problem with the stove, but that should be okay now."

"What was wrong with it?"

"I spilled water on it and it didn't work for a while."

"Jah, sometimes they need to dry out when that happens."

For the first time, Evelyn was curious how Hezekiah had managed to look after his household and *kinner* without a wife. When Jane had died, she hadn't gone over and offered her help. She'd left it up to others in the community and right now Evelyn was disappointed in herself. Next time someone in the community died, she'd make an effort to see how the family was coping. She only hoped she'd be in a position to help when that happened; right now she would be no help.

She was reminded of the Scripture that she'd read the night before. "Is there anything I can help you with, Hezekiah? Things must have changed for you since Jane died."

"It was hard at first but we all pitch in and do what Jane used to do. *Nee denke,* we're fine." He finished the last of his coffee. "I'll get those logs in for you and you'll be warm tonight."

She stood too. "I'll help."

"Me too," Martha said.

He laughed and then leaned forward and touched Martha on her head. "You stay and eat your breakfast." He looked back at Evelyn. "I don't need help."

When he'd brought the last of the wood in, he stepped outside and they said their goodbyes while Martha hung onto her mother's apron. They both turned their heads when they saw a buggy coming toward them.

"Looks like Mark," Evelyn said recognizing the horse.

"I'll wait to say hello."

It wasn't Mark. As the buggy drew closer, they could both see only one person in the buggy and that person was Jed.

"Oh, it's Mark and Sally's visitor, Jed," Evelyn said, now feeling awkward.

Jed got out of the buggy and the two men introduced themselves while Evelyn stayed near the door. She overheard their conversation.

"You're Hezekiah? My real name's Jebediah!" Jed laughed. "Now all we need is a Nehemiah, a Jeremiah and a... Well, never mind."

Hezekiah remained stony-faced as he turned to wave to Evelyn.

Jed walked over to her. "Morning, Evelyn."

"Morning, Jed."

When Hezekiah drove away, Jed said, "I take it that's the man you're *not* going to marry?"

Evelyn's mouth fell open. "He was splitting wood for me." She bit her lip when she realized how bad that sounded, as though she was using the man to do things for her. "He dropped by unexpectedly and offered to do that. I didn't ask."

Jed laughed. "No need to explain anything to me."

Of course, there wouldn't be a need to explain herself. *Jed is marrying someone else; why would he care what I'm doing, or what Hezekiah's doing?* "I didn't mean for you to overhear what I said about him."

"I won't tell anyone. You're secret's safe with me."

"It's not a secret. I don't have secrets." She stopped her sentence abruptly. She did have secrets. Now she had the secret that she owed Hezekiah money, thanks to Amos. "Did Mark send you here?"

"He did, but I can see I'm too late."

Evelyn frowned.

"I came here to see that you had enough firewood. Mark and Sally thought you might be running low."

Martha moved forward and held onto one of Jed's legs.

Evelyn pulled her away. "Martha! You can't do that."

Jed laughed. "It's okay," he said as he lifted her up onto his shoulders as her loud giggles rang out.

"Run!" Martha called out, wanting him to run with her on his shoulders as he'd done the previous day.

"Nee, I've come to see what I can do for your *mudder* today." He looked over at Evelyn. "I'm at your service today. I've nothing to do and Mark's gone to work. You'll be doing me a favor if you give me things to do."

She shook her head. "I can't pay you. I would if I could, but I can't."

"I've not asked for any payment. I meant it when I said you'd be doing me a favor."

Maybe God was answering her prayers. "How much work would you like?"

"Whatever you've got. I can work until sunset."

Until dark? Evelyn tapped a finger on her chin. The

jobs she had to do were large jobs that would take many days. There were plaster repairs, repairs to the floorboards, and the windows didn't shut properly.

"You could clean the gutters out for me."

"I'd love to do that."

Evelyn giggled. "There's a ladder in the barn."

"While I do that, come up with something else for me to do."

"I will. I'll have a long list just like the one you made for William's *haus.*"

Jed laughed and placed Martha back on the ground. "We might be allowed to play later, but first, I've got work to do."

"Okay," Martha said staring up at him.

"While you have the ladder out, you could clean the windows on the upper level of the house."

He nodded. "Certainly."

"I'll get the water and the bucket ready."

As he strode off to the barn, Evelyn hurried to get the bucket and the window-cleaning items ready for him. They always cleaned their windows with Methylated Spirits. She was embarrassed that he'd see how long it had been since the gutters and the windows were cleaned.

After three hours of work, Evelyn managed to convince Jed to take a break so he could eat. She'd made a pie and a pot roast and roasted vegetables. Martha was taking her afternoon nap.

"I guess you can tell that the place hasn't had any attention for some time."

"I noticed. Was Amos sick before he died?"

"*Nee.* He might have felt poorly but he never let on to me that he did. After he died, the doctor told me that he could've had feelings of depression, anxiety and general unhappiness."

"Did you notice he had these feelings? If you don't mind me asking."

Evelyn sighed. "I knew something was wrong, but I didn't know it was something so dangerous." Evelyn swallowed hard and said, "I've only just found out that he lost his job a whole year ago."

"He never told you?"

Evelyn shook her head.

"Did he leave every day and go somewhere?"

Now she would have to tell him of their living arrangements.

She shook her head and looked away.

"You don't have to answer. It seems strange that you wouldn't know."

"Amos didn't spend much time here. He spent most of his time at his *vadder's haus.*"

Jed looked away and nodded. "I thought that might've been the case when I saw the bedroom. It looked as though someone had been living there. And there was paperwork with his name on it. I didn't like to mention it to you."

Now that she'd told someone it didn't seem so shameful. Evelyn sniffed.

"It must've been hard on you."

"It was and on Martha. Now I know why he never played with her and never stayed here at the *haus* often."

"You say he hadn't worked in a year?"

"That's right. A whole year." She shook her head. "You know, I haven't told anyone what I've just told you."

"Maybe you should. Everything's easier when you share your troubles with people."

"I can't help feeling ashamed, as though I could've done something to prevent what happened. His death, him losing his job, the way he was…"

"Things happen how they're meant to occur. Sometimes bad things happen and we can't avoid them—like a pothole in the road that we don't see until we're upon it. It's too late to turn the buggy and we have to close our eyes and hope the wheels don't fall off."

Evelyn laughed. "Life potholes?"

He nodded. "Potholes on the road of life."

"That's a nice way to see things." Evelyn felt better. "Would you like seconds?"

"Nee. I'd better get back to work so I'll have time to play with Martha before it gets dark."

CHAPTER 10

The Lord is slow to anger and abounding in steadfast love,
forgiving iniquity and transgression,
but he will by no means clear the guilty,
visiting the iniquity of the fathers on the children,
to the third and the fourth generation
Numbers 14:18

THE NEXT DAY, Beth, her oldest sister came to visit.

"You need to be able to ask people to help you. No one will know that you need help if you don't reach out."

"Mark's visitor, Jed, helped me with things yesterday. I allowed him to help."

"Gut!"

"Anyway, I'm managing fine at the moment. Mark is figuring out what to do with the *haus*—with William's *haus*." Her sister kept glaring at her, so she added, "I don't like to bother people."

"If someone asked you for help would you give it?"

"Of course, I would."

"And you'd feel good about it?"

"Well, yes. I like to help others." Evelyn smiled.

"You need to let others feel good by being able to receive as well as give. It's an action that goes two ways."

"It's just that everybody seems so busy all the time."

"That's only because people like to keep busy." Beth looked about her. "I can see now why you haven't invited anybody over these past couple of years. How did Amos let the place get into a state like this?"

"He had William's *haus* to look after as well and he was sick even though he never let on. I suppose he found it too hard to keep up the repair of the two places."

Beth folded her arms over her chest. "From what Sally told me, William's house was in a dreadful state."

Evelyn yawned.

"What's wrong?"

"I'm tired, that's all. I feel everything is piling on top of me."

"That's why you need to reach out to people and ask for help. With you being the youngest, I would've thought you'd be used to having people do things for you." Beth laughed at her own words.

"*Denke* for watching Martha. She loves playing with Jemima."

"They're like sisters more than cousins. Sally tells me that Hezekiah asked you to marry him."

Evelyn gasped. "She should never have told anybody that."

"Why can't I know if Sally knows? I'm your *schweschder* too. Anyway, she only told me—no one else."

"I had to tell someone and Sally was the next person I saw right after he asked me. Are you certain Sally won't tell anyone else?"

"Nee she won't. We were talking about you and she just mentioned how you were feeling down in the dumps and then she just happened to mention that Hezekiah asked you to marry him." Beth gave a small giggle.

I wish I'd never mentioned anything. I'll really feel bad if that gets back to Hezekiah."

"Well, what did you say to him?"

"What do you mean what did I say to him? Of course, I wouldn't marry him, he's too old for me and he's not right for me."

"Amos was older than you."

"Not that much older. He was only eight years older, not a hundred years older than I am."

Beth giggled. "I think Hezekiah would be about twenty years older. His first wife, Jane, was younger than he was too."

"Don't say 'first wife' as though I'm going to be his second."

"Maybe it is something you should seriously consider."

"*Nee!* I don't feel that way about him."

"You might if you spent some time with him and got to know him better."

"He's too serious for me. And I don't care so much about his age physically, it's more his age mentally. He seems so much older. Do you see what I mean?"

Beth shook her head. "I don't. You'd have a good life with him. I think you should consider it. He's quite a wealthy man and if you married him you wouldn't have a care in the world."

"If I ever marry again, I'm going to marry for love. I feel as though I was forced into my marriage with Amos; everyone told me that love would develop. Instead, things went from here to here." With a hand, she gestured high then low.

"Are you blaming me?" Beth asked.

"I'm not blaming anybody."

"Because I think I told you that you would fall in love with him after you married. I felt more deeply in love with Ronald after we were married. Sorry if I said anything to steer you in the wrong direction. I would never want to do that.

"I'm not blaming anybody. It was my decision to make. I can't blame anybody for that. It was some older ladies in the community that swayed my decision. I thought I should marry or I'd be on my own forever. I kept waiting but nobody had shown up." Jed came into Evelyn's mind and she couldn't help but smile.

"Why are you smiling? Have you met someone?"

"I'm only smiling because I've had a bad few days. I'm smiling because it's a little trick I do to make myself feel better."

"Is there anything I can do for you?"

Evelyn shook her head. "I'm all cried out. I have no more tears left. I'll think about what you said about asking people for help. I don't know why I have such a problem with it."

"Do you feel unworthy; is that it? Maybe you feel that you're not worthy enough for people to help, or to take up their time?"

"I don't know."

"Why don't you talk things over with the bishop?"

"I'm not the kind of person who runs to the bishop with every little problem I have. Besides, it wouldn't give anybody else any time to talk with him—people with bigger problems."

"Maybe your problem is that you're stubborn."

"I could be. I'm just trying to have faith and live day to day."

"Along with faith must come action. You can't sit and believe that *Gott* will do something for you when you're doing nothing to help yourself." She raised her arms in the air. "I'm not saying that's the case with you, I'm just saying that if you can do something toward whatever it is that you want to have, then that's what you should do."

Again, Evelyn's mind drifted back to the story of the widow. In faith she made Elijah the bread as he instructed. Maybe she had to make a step in faith.

"What are you thinking about?" Beth asked.

"I'm thinking about what you said and it doesn't make sense. I have to act in faith, but how do I know what *Gott* wants me to do in faith?"

"The community always lends a hand, so just ask someone when you want something done. It's that simple. You don't have to think so hard and worry so much about things."

Beth assumed she was talking about practical things, but Evelyn was talking about things of the heart. She'd like nothing more than to fall in love and marry a man who loved her.

"Okay, then, I'll ask you if you can mind Martha later today. I have a few errands to run and it'll be faster without her."

"Of course I will. She'll love to play with Jemima when she gets out of *schul*."

"*Denke*."

"I can take her with me now."

"Perfect. This 'asking people for things' really works." Evelyn giggled.

"You've never had any problem asking me for anything. It's other people you have a problem with."

Evelyn nodded.

CHAPTER 11

The Lord is slow to anger and great in power, and the Lord will
by no means clear the guilty.
His way is in whirlwind and storm,
and the clouds are the dust of his feet.
Nahum 1:3

BETH TOOK Martha back home with her when she left Evelyn's place, as Evelyn had to go into town. On her way, Evelyn stopped at Sally's house hoping Mark would be home so she could discuss selling Amos' buggy horse. Then she would drive to the bank to close down her husband's account.

When she got down from the buggy, Jed came out of the barn and waved to her. "They're not here," he said as he walked closer.

Evelyn stayed by her horse's shoulder. "I was hoping Mark would be here."

"Do you need help with something?"

"I have to put Amos' horse into auction." She pointed to the tall black horse in the paddock.

Jed turned to look and then smiled at her. "He's a good looking horse."

Evelyn nodded. "Amos liked horses."

"Why don't you keep him and sell your other horse?"

"Nee. I'm used to this one." She patted her horse's neck. "I'd get more money for the black one. I think Amos paid quite a bit for him just six months ago. He said he cost more because of the way he looks." Once she'd uttered the words she realized that Amos had used Hezekiah's money to buy the black horse. She was annoyed that he'd have done such a thing.

"You might do well from the auction, then."

"I hope so." Remembering what her sister said about asking, she said, "What are you doing right now?"

"Nothing. Just trying to fill up my time until Mark gets home. They'll be another two hours."

"Perhaps you'd drive me to talk to the auctioneers and then drive me to the bank?"

"I'd be happy to." He leaned over and looked into the back of the buggy. "You're by yourself?"

"My sister, Beth, is minding Martha while I go into town."

He jumped up into the buggy. "I'm driving."

Evelyn giggled. "Okay."

"Oh, do you need help?" he said to her as she climbed into the buggy.

"I'm fine."

He turned the buggy around and they headed toward the road.

"You've got a lot of *familye* here?" he asked.

"*Jah,* I'm the youngest of nine girls. Sally is the second youngest and I suppose that's why we're close. It's handy that she lives close by too. My oldest *schweschder* is Beth, and she's the one who's minding Martha. What about yourself? Do you come from a large family?"

"There are five of us brothers, and I'm the one in the middle. I'm the only one not married."

"But you'll be married soon."

"I hope so."

"What's her name?" Evelyn asked.

"Mary Jones."

Evelyn nodded and tried to hide her disappointment at hearing a name. Up until now, she'd hoped that there wasn't a fiancée, and maybe he had said he was getting married soon simply because he hoped to get married. "That's a nice name—Mary."

"*Jah,* it's a *gut* name."

"Is she from Ohio too?"

"*Jah,* she is."

"Nice."

"*Jah.*" He looked over at her and smiled.

Why was it that she felt this connection? The man was soon to marry someone else. "Have you been to our county before?"

"When I was younger I visited. I stayed with the bishop back then. He's my *onkel.*"

"Oh, I didn't know that. I don't know much about the bishop's relatives."

"He's not really a close *onkel,* we're distantly related. My father's aunt is his cousin, or some such thing." He laughed. "I can never keep track of who is related to who."

"I have that problem too."

"I never asked you before, but how is Martha coping without her *vadder?*"

"She doesn't really understand."

"She seems to have a liking for Mr. Hofstetter."

Evelyn laughed. "You said his name just like she says it. *Jah,* she does like him. He's a kind man."

Jed glanced over at her, momentarily taking his eyes from the road.

"What?"

"Since you told me so much about yourself yesterday, I owe it to tell you something about myself."

Evelyn stared at him waiting for him to continue.

"I have no woman that I'm going to marry."

Evelyn sat there stunned. What reason would he have for lying to everyone? "There's no Mary?"

"There is a Mary. There's a Mary that everyone thinks I should marry, the way it might make sense for some that you marry Hezekiah."

Finally, Evelyn understood a little better. "But why tell us that you're engaged to be married when it's not true?"

"For the simple reason that each time I go to a different community, people find single women to introduce me to. People automatically think I'm there looking for a wife when I'm not. I like to move around and see different parts of the country."

Evelyn knew what he said was true. People would try to match him with a suitable wife once they learned that he was a single man.

"What you're saying makes sense, but what if Mary hears back that you're telling people that you're going to marry her?"

He laughed. "I never mention a name to anyone. No one has ever asked me about her, except for you." He glanced over at her. "Most people only want to talk about themselves and that shows me that you're not a selfish person."

Evelyn gave a little laugh. "Sometimes I am."

He shook his head. "I can't believe you have any faults."

And there it was—the warm fuzzy feeling that Evelyn had waited all her life to feel.

"Mary's a close friend even though she's years younger. She lives on the farm next to ours. She's like my young *schweschder* and I don't feel a marriage between us would be the best thing for either of us."

"How does she feel?"

"Mary's quite outspoken about her feelings. She said she'd only marry a man with brown eyes and dark hair."

Evelyn giggled. "It's good that she knows what she wants. Do you feel rejected?"

He laughed. "I suppose if I were in love with her, I'd be very upset. Her parents are pressuring us to marry, which is the real reason I'm here. We both—Mary and I— thought if I went away for a few months that would take the pressure off."

"So that's why you're here?"

"*Jah,* but you're the only person who knows." He put his finger to his mouth to signal 'sh.' "I haven't even told Mark. You know how news travels around the communities like wildfire."

"I know. I'm glad you told me, and your secret's safe with me."

"Now we hold each other's secrets. I know that

Hezekiah asked you to marry him, and now you know why I'm here."

"That's a fair exchange."

They came to a fork in the road.

"You'll have to direct me from here."

"Go left," Evelyn said.

"Do you know how much you want for the horse?"

"Nee, I don't. I'll book him in and see what their process is. I'd keep him but I don't think I'd need two horses. If mine goes lame, I can always have Mark and Sally drive me places until he recovers."

"That's the best way," he said looking out into the fields.

"Do you like it here?"

He smiled at her. "I'm liking it more every day."

After Jed took her to all the auctioneers and then the bank, the last stop was the supermarket. With the money left in Amos' account, there was enough food for a month's worth of groceries. Since she didn't want to hold Jed up too much, she only bought the weekly necessities.

He followed her around the supermarket pushing the shopping cart. Amos had never gone to the supermarket with her; it was nice to have a man shop with her. Once he loaded the groceries into the buggy, he suggested that they find somewhere to have lunch. She agreed.

They found a diner up the road from the supermarket.

She opened the menu after they were seated. "I can't remember the last time I ate out."

"Didn't Amos take you out to eat? Many people in the community back home eat out nowadays."

"I know it wouldn't have happened years ago, but now they even go through the drive though section of the fast-food outlets in their buggies. To answer your question, Amos never liked to eat out. He liked to eat at home and his food had to be exactly how his *mudder* made it." It'd been exhausting and awful, but Evelyn didn't tell Jed that or she would've sounded rude.

"Did he ever compliment your food, or say thank you for the effort you'd gone to?"

"He did if I'd made it just like his *mudder,* but he was a man of few words. And I don't think he was being rude or uncaring, it was just that he wasn't that interested in food. Maybe it all tasted the same to him—I don't know. To be fair, I never thanked him for his contribution to our *familye,* for working so hard. I never thought to thank him—I just expected him to do it."

"I've never been married, but I hope when I marry that I will appreciate my *fraa* every single day because she'll be a very smart woman." He laughed.

Evelyn gave a little laugh at his humor, and then hunger drew her eyes back to the menu.

He opened his menu. "Let's see now. I think I'll go with the hamburger and fries."

"I was about to say the same."

When they closed the menus, the waitress took their order.

"I hope you're not going to be late to see Mark. Did you have something planned for this afternoon?"

"He's visiting people to see how many people we can find to work on your *haus* over the next few weeks."

"Really?"

"*Jah.*"

"That's good of him, but I didn't know I had agreed to that."

"There's no reason not to. We all help each other. There's nothing wrong with reaching out and taking someone's hand when you can't see in the dark."

"Well the next horse auction is not for another month and I'll have to rely on Mark or one of my other *bruder*-in-laws to get the horse there. I don't like to ask people to do too many things."

"No one will mind. People want to do things for you. We're all a *familye*." He smiled at her. "One week you help someone, the next week they're helping you."

Evelyn nodded. "I know. Sally tells me things like that all the time. It's hard for me to accept help, or to ask for it."

"You give help though, don't you?"

"I would, if someone asked me. But I don't think I've helped too many people and that's something I've been thinking about lately." Evelyn laughed. "I don't know why I'm telling you so much about myself. I normally don't speak about myself so much."

"I'm glad you're telling me about yourself. I want to get to know you better."

CHAPTER 12

But the fruit of the Spirit is love, joy, peace, patience, kindness,
goodness,
faithfulness, gentleness, self-control;
against such things there is no law.
Galatians 5:22-23

BEFORE EVELYN HAD GONE home that day, Sally had insisted she'd have Jed bring Amos' buggy to her house. The buggy Amos had been using was in better repair than the old one Evelyn had been using. It made perfect sense for her to use the good one. Mark had taken the horse and buggy from William's house for safekeeping not long after Amos had died.

Knowing she'd be getting a visitor that day—Jed—Evelyn had been on a cleaning frenzy. If the house looked clean and tidy it wouldn't look so drab and in need of repair.

"He's here, *Mamm*."

Evelyn rushed to the window where Martha had been waiting for their visitor. *"Gut,* now hold my hand and we can go out to meet him. I must thank him for bringing the buggy here. Now remember, his name is Mr. Esh."

"Okay."

When he looked over, he said, *"Guder Mariye."*

"Guder Mariye." Evelyn replied while Martha ducked behind her, hanging on to her mother's dress.

"Where would you like the buggy?"

"Just in the barn next to the old one, *denke.* I suppose I could've changed buggies while I was there yesterday, but that would've left the old buggy at their place."

"Mark said not to bring your black horse, just the buggy."

"You could've brought my horse and we could've led him back. I'm taking you back to Mark's place anyway."

"Mark said this horse needed the exercise, and he didn't want to risk the other getting injured before the auction."

Evelyn nodded. "He's got so many horses I lose track of them."

Jed jumped down and led the horse closer to the barn.

"Hello, Mr. Esh."

He stopped and looked over. "Hello, Martha. I didn't notice you there."

"I was hiding." She giggled.

"That's her favorite game at the moment."

"That was one of my favorites too."

"Will you play?"

He stopped and looked over at Evelyn. "I don't know if

we'll have the time today." He raised his eyebrows and looked at Evelyn.

"It depends if you have the time. We don't want to hold you up from anything."

"I'll put the buggy away, tie the horse and I'll come and tell you what I've got planned for your *vadder*-in-law's *haus*."

She smiled and nodded, but realized that meant he would need to come inside the house. It was far too cold to discuss matters on the porch and it would seem rude. "I'll boil the pot for a cup of tea."

"Denke, just what I need. It'll warm me."

"Come on, Martha." She held Martha's hand and turned to go inside.

"I want to play."

"Mr. Esh is coming inside to speak with me and he might play with you after that, but only if you're quiet while he's talking to me."

"Okay, *Mamm.*" Martha let out a sigh.

That was the first time she'd heard Martha made such a noise and she was well aware that Martha had picked up on her tendency to sigh. Evelyn knew she'd have to stop doing that.

Evelyn set Martha up on a blanket with toys and then put the pot on to boil. She hadn't had anyone fix the leaking tap yet and had been using the more easily accessible rainwater tank that was originally supposed to be used for the livestock. The tank for the household was designed to go straight into the house pipes and if there were an outside access point, Evelyn had no idea how to find it.

Jed settled himself at the kitchen table. "Because of the time of year, Mark couldn't find many people to work on your *haus*. You'll be doing me a favor if you'll allow me to fix the house for you. It might take some time, but it won't cost you. Mark will be able to take time off and, between the two of us, we can do the bulk of it in a few days."

"Why would you do this when you're saving for a house? Wouldn't you be better off doing paid work somewhere?"

"*Nee*. My situation is nothing for you to concern yourself with. And I don't mean that in a rude way," Jed said with a chuckle. "I came here for a change of scene and I'd be happy if you would allow me to do work for you and bring the *haus* back to what it was."

"Are you certain you want to do this? I can pay you in time."

He shook his head. "Not necessary. Between Mark and me, we'll organize materials and see what we can get for nothing. People have offered materials already."

"That's so *gut* of them. All right, *denke,* I'd be happy for you and Mark to look after things for me at the *haus.*"

"*Gut!* Now where's that cup of tea? And then you'll have to take me back in the buggy."

Evelyn smiled, stood up and filled the teapot.

"I guess I shouldn't have unhitched it. If you take me back then you'll have to unhitch the buggy by yourself when you get back. I'll walk back. It won't take me long."

"*Nee* you can't do that. It's too cold."

"It's not that far at all and I'll jog to keep warm."

"What about Mark's horse?"

"Ah! I could jump on his back and hopefully he's been trained for a saddle."

Evelyn giggled as she lit the stove. "If he hasn't been, you'll have to hang on."

"Jah, I might get home quicker than I expected." Jed laughed.

CHAPTER 13

Put on then, as God's chosen ones, holy and beloved,
compassionate hearts,
kindness, humility, meekness, and patience,
bearing with one another and,
if one has a complaint against another,
forgiving each other; as the Lord has forgiven you,
so you also must forgive.
Colossians 3:12-13

AFTER LEAVING Martha with her oldest sister, Beth, Evelyn headed to Sally's house, as Sally was going to take her to her appointment with the midwife. When Sally's house came into view, she knew she would be too late to see Jed; she kept looking and hoping he might be there.

Before she could knock on the door, Sally flung it open.

"It's been a long time since we've both been child-free." Sally said smiling as Evelyn walked in.

"It has been. I can't recall the last time I had someone mind Martha; she normally goes to visit Dana with me." The sound of the crackling fire made Evelyn feel as though she didn't want to go anywhere; rather she wanted to stay right in front of the fire with a cup of tea. That would be the nicest thing.

"Best she stays with Beth and doesn't go with you from now on. You're getting close to the end and you need to focus on this birth." Sally reached over and patted Evelyn's stomach, which made Evelyn laugh. "Come and warm yourself by the fire."

Evelyn hung her shawl behind the door and walked over to the crackling fire.

"I'll pull a chair close for you."

"Denke," When Sally had moved the chair Evelyn sat down, and then Sally pushed another one near the fire for herself.

"Cup of tea?"

"Nee denke, I just had one."

"That doesn't usually stop you."

"That's true, but I'm a little nervous about the appointment. I'm not sure why."

"Probably because this is the first time you've gone to see the midwife since Amos died."

"That could be it." Evelyn held her hands up to the fire. "Where's Jed today?"

"I'm not certain if he's working on your *haus* or someone else's *haus* today. Do you want to drive past your house when your appointment is over?"

"Nee."

"What is it?"

"Nothing."

"You like him, don't you?"

"He's a nice man and he seems kind. That's all I'm saying."

"Why? We tell each other everything." When Evelyn remained silent, Sally probed further. "Are you keeping something from me?"

"I told you about Hezekiah."

"Jah, I know but I've got a feeling you're keeping something else from me."

Evelyn sighed and then told her about Amos' large debt to Hezekiah. When she'd finished explaining, Sally looked white in the face.

"You should've told me right away."

Evelyn shook her head. "There's nothing you can do about it. Nothing anyone can do about it."

Sally raised her eyebrows. "If you marry Hezekiah, you won't have a thing to worry about."

Evelyn shook her head. "I hate to say it but sometimes it sounds tempting. I've always gotten along well with his *kinner,* they're lovely."

"Jah, they're delightful. But you can't marry someone for those reasons."

"I married Amos for less."

Sally frowned, and muttered, "That was a long time ago."

"It doesn't make any difference. I still should never have married Amos. He seemed nice and I thought love would grow, but it didn't. Things just got worse. In the end, I don't think he even liked me."

"Of course he did."

Evelyn shook her head. "It makes little difference if he did or didn't. If I ever marry again it must be for love." She stared into her sister's face. "Tell me what it feels like to be in love."

Sally's face glowed as her gaze turned upward. "I feel excited when I know he's going to be coming home soon —I can scarcely wait. All the time, I want to be near him. He makes me happy when he's around and even when he's not around, just thinking about him makes me smile. My life is much better since we married." She looked back at Evelyn. "Does that explain it?"

"The look on your face explains it better."

Sally giggled. "It's hard to put feelings into words. You'll know when you're in love. You won't have to ask anyone if you're in love."

"So, if I have to ask someone if I'm in love, I'll know I'm not?"

"That's right. You'll know it in your heart because you'll want to be near him all the time."

"I hope I find someone like that one day. My biggest regret is not having my *kinner* with a man I was in love with. I feel almost like I've been cheated."

"Don't feel like that. *Gott* might have planned it that way so your *kinner* could come into the world. Think about it, if Amos didn't come into your life, you wouldn't have had Martha or Tom."

"Tom?"

Sally giggled. "That's what I'm calling him."

Evelyn placed a hand over her stomach. "I might have a girl."

"I think he'll be a boy."

"I don't know that I like the name Tom. I guess I don't dislike it, but I don't think that'll be my *boppli's* name."

"We've got a few weeks to think of something. Now if we were to go to a doctor and you were to have an ultrasound, you'd know if you were having a boy or a girl and that would make finding a name easier."

"Not this again! I told you I'm having a home-birth and that's all there is to it."

"You know she's not trained."

"I know that. She's been delivering babies in the community for twenty years just like her mother before her. You can train someone but you can't train a person into having instincts. That's all the training I need her to have— and she delivered Martha. Her mother delivered all of us."

"I know that, but wouldn't you feel better if you went to a doctor and just checked out that there was nothing wrong?"

"Sounds like you're expecting things to go wrong."

"Nee I'm not, but I felt a whole lot better when I went to a doctor for my second birth."

"I wouldn't. I don't like doctors at all, not one little bit. All they want to do is give medicine to treat the symptoms rather than look further to see what's causing the problem."

Sally giggled.

"What's funny?"

"Nothing."

"There's nothing funny about visiting doctors. Anything that's wrong with me I can take herbs for."

Sally sighed. "There are all kinds of things that can go wrong."

"*Jah,* but I'm certain if doctors get involved there might be more things that they can cause to go wrong. Dana says the more the doctors intervene, the more things that can go wrong. It's proven to be correct and Dana's studied the statistics."

"It suits Dana to say things like that. Anyone can twist things with statistics to suit themselves."

"No they can't. The numbers don't lie. I've heard some horror stories of what happens. I prefer to have my *boppli* at home. If there's an emergency, the hospital's not far away."

"Okay. I do have to say Dana's experienced, I'll give her that much. We better go now if you don't want to be late." Sally passed Evelyn her shawl and then wrapped her own over her shoulders. "Mark hitched the buggy already."

"We could've taken my buggy." Evelyn followed Sally out the door.

"Mark didn't want us to go in your buggy. He said to let you know you shouldn't travel long distances in it if you're still using the old one."

"I'm using the newer one today. I won't use the old one again. *Denke,* for having Jed bring it to me. I've got people doing things for me, but I haven't done anything for anyone for a long time. I want to do something to help someone."

"You're doing something helpful by raising Martha and looking after Tom."

"I never thought of it like that."

"And you mix up your potions to give people when they're sick, and you're always giving people your teas when they fall ill."

"I haven't done anything with my herbs for weeks and I haven't even been outside to water them. Everything has fallen by the wayside since Amos died. I do feel better when I'm mixing up things for people."

"That's what you're good at. *Gott* gave you that gift. Now let's go. It's a good twenty minutes away."

"I'm right behind you."

The sisters glanced at one another and exchanged smiles. Sally always made Evelyn feel better through her encouraging words.

CHAPTER 14

For in this hope we were saved Now hope that is seen is not hope. For who hopes for what he sees? But if we hope for what we do not see, we wait for it with patience.
Romans 8: 24-25

OVER THE NEXT FOUR WEEKS, Evelyn visited her house almost every day to watch the progress Jed was making. As well as Mark, there were other Amish men helping with the project. Members of the community had donated building materials as well as their labor.

After she hadn't been to the house for several days, Jed knocked on her door.

Evelyn opened the door to see his concerned face.

"Are you alright? You haven't been to the *haus* for days."

"Come in." As soon as he walked in, she said, "I'm okay, just a little tired. Have a seat. Are you hungry?"

"I'm always hungry."

"I've just made a pot roast. On second thought, let's go into the kitchen and I'll slice you some."

"It smells *wunderbaar.*"

"Well, I hope it tastes as *gut.*"

"Where is Martha?"

"She's asleep. Sometimes she still has an afternoon nap."

When she'd placed a bowl of food in front of him, she sat opposite. "How's the *haus* going?"

"It's making gut progress. I've had a couple of ladies, Olive and Greta, come out to look at the garden. They're going to plant something out in front." Jed chuckled. "I was too busy to listen to what they were saying. They were speaking mostly to Mark."

"That's so kind of them. I'll be sure to thank them."

"They heard you were getting the old placed fixed up." He took another mouthful. "Mmm. This is tasty."

"*Denke.* Maybe you should slow down."

He laughed. "I'm hungrier than I thought."

"That's because I didn't bring food out to you today. I'm sorry."

Since he had a mouthful, he shook his head and waved his hand. When he'd finished swallowing he said, "You've got better things to do than run after me."

"Would you like more?"

He shook his head. *"Nee denke.* That was enough. I meant to tell you, Mark and I took your horse to the auction this morning. He had to be there two days before the auction took place."

"*Denke.* I didn't realize it was going to be happening so soon."

"How about you come with me and we'll watch the auction? Just you and me; we could make a day of it."

"I would, but I think it'd be too tiring for Martha."

"We could leave her with one of your *schweschders* on the way."

A smile slowly crept across her face at the thought of a whole day alone with Jed. "I'd love to. I'm sure Beth wouldn't mind and Martha loves going to Beth's *haus.*"

"That's settled then. I'll borrow one of Mark's buggies and I'll collect you early in the morning. How about we go for breakfast first?"

Delighted with the attention he was paying her, Evelyn nodded.

He leaned toward her with his blue eyes sparkling. "I'll look forward to it."

"Me too."

"I've got a few things to tie up at the *haus* before I finish for the day." He looked about him. "Seems very quiet with Martha asleep."

"It is peaceful."

He stood. "Can I do anything for you while I'm here?"

She glanced up at the ceiling. "I do have a fear of spiders and there are two cobwebs in the corners up there." She pointed. "I haven't seen the spiders, but they must be around somewhere."

"I'll get them for you."

"*Denke,* I would've got them down myself, but I only just noticed them earlier today."

"They can appear in a day. It takes them no time at all to spin a web."

Evelyn shuddered at the thought. "I'll get the broom."

"I'll get it; just tell me where it is."

"Just outside the back door."

Minutes later the cobwebs were gone.

He glanced at the dishes in the sink. "I'll do those before I go. You sit down."

"I can't let you."

"I insist. That's the least I can do for you."

Evelyn sat at the kitchen table hoping the tap wouldn't act up. It was strange that a man was washing up. She'd never seen her father or Amos lift a finger in the kitchen —that was looked upon as women's work. "Do you know what you're doing?" she said with a laugh.

He turned around and flashed her a smile. "I do, and if you keep up that talk I'll make you a beard." He picked up the bubbles in the sink.

Evelyn giggled. "Put them on yourself. We'll see what you'll look like when you're married."

He scooped up bubbles and dabbed them on his face to make a beard. "How do I look?" As he faced her, she broke into peals of laughter. "Handsome?" he asked.

"Very handsome. I only wish someone would knock on the door; then I'd make you answer it."

He laughed and turned to continue washing up with soap bubbles still on his face. "I hope this is rejuvenating for my skin," he said as he scrubbed the plates.

"You'll be clean."

Evelyn stood to put the bowls away once he was finished. Seeing the bubbles still on his face she picked up a dishtowel and said, "Turn to me."

When he faced her, she dabbed at his handsome face. It'd been some time since she'd been so close to a man. She stepped back when she'd finished even though she wanted to stay close to him.

"Denke," he said in a husky tone. When she lifted her hand to put the dishtowel down, he took hold of her hand and pulled her close. "Evelyn, would you ever marry again?"

She swallowed hard and stared into the bluest of blue eyes. How she wanted him to sweep her into his arms and hold her tight.

He added, "If you found a man to marry."

Nervous, she pulled her hand away. "I would."

He cleared his throat. "Before I go I'll take a look at that fire."

"I've got plenty of chopped wood."

Once Jed walked into the living room, he leaned down, put another log on, and then straightened up. "That should last a while."

"Denke, Jed. You're always so helpful."

"You make me want to do things for you." He stepped toward her but she stepped back. Wagging a finger at her, he said, "Don't forget I'll be here to collect you bright and early on Friday."

Her face beamed with the thought of spending a whole day with him, and just him. "I'm looking forward to it, and I'll be ready."

When he left, she looked out the window at him driving away. She was certain that he was fond of her, and he certainly liked Martha. Would he really be interested in her? It felt nice to have a man around the house.

FRIDAY MORNING finally arrived and Evelyn had Martha packed and ready to stay at her aunt Beth's house.

"He's here; he's here," Martha called out excitedly.

"Okay, are you all ready? Have we got everything?"

"Jah."

Evelyn picked up Martha's bag, which contained a change of clothing, and opened the front door. Once she closed it behind her, she managed to grab Martha's hand before she ran to the buggy.

Jed jumped down. *"Guder mariye."*

"Guder mariye."

"Hello, Mr. Esh," Martha said in a small voice.

"Hello, Martha. Are you ready to go to your aunt's *haus?"*

Martha nodded.

He scooped Martha up and placed her on the back seat with her bag, and then helped Evelyn into the buggy.

Once they'd dropped Martha at Beth's house, they were finally alone.

"I've been looking forward to today," he said.

"Me too."

"What? Being with me, or the horse auction?"

"Breakfast," she said with a smile.

He laughed. *"Denke,* I hope we can improve on that."

He took her to the diner they'd already been to.

"I noticed when we were here before that their breakfast menu looked good."

Studying the menu from their table by the window, Evelyn had to agree. "It does look nice. I'll have to go with the bacon, scrambled eggs and hash browns."

"Sounds gut. I'm going with the big breakfast."

After the waitress had taken their orders, she filled their coffee cups. Evelyn had stopped drinking coffee months ago, but the waitress didn't even ask if she wanted it. Evelyn suddenly felt nervous; she'd grown to like Jed so much, but didn't know what to do, what to say, or how to act around him.

"I must say, I always like spending time with you."

"Me too. You make me laugh."

He smiled. "That's something you should do more often. Your whole face lights up when you laugh. Sometimes you look so sad."

"I am sad sometimes."

"You should never be sad. You've got so much going for you."

"I have?"

He nodded and took a mouthful of coffee. "You've got a *dochder*, another child on the way, and a *familye* who love you. You've also got two houses, when many people don't even have one."

Evelyn stared into her coffee that she wasn't going to drink. He was right. She hadn't appreciated exactly what she had—she'd been too busy looking at the way she thought things should be.

"You're absolutely right. *Gott* must have sent you here to scold me."

He laughed. "I don't know about that. I wasn't scolding you—just be happy. There's no reason to be otherwise. You're probably thinking that I don't know what it feels like to lose a spouse and that's true, but I've had loss in my life."

"Your parents?"

He nodded. "And I had a sister who was born not long after my youngest *bruder*. She died when she was two and I don't think my parents ever recovered."

"That's sad, I didn't know."

"It's a part of life and I always thought it was cold when I heard people say that, but it's true. One day we'll be gone."

"That's a cheery thought. Didn't you want me to smile?"

Jed took a mouthful of coffee. "We've so little time here on earth that we should make the best of it and that's living it with a smile—thinking of others more than ourselves. I used to be critical of others when I was younger until I learned that there's always a reason why people behave the way they do. Often it's because they've been hurt, and I don't mean physically."

"I know what you mean. Amos could've acted like he did because he *was* sick." She shrugged her shoulders. "It's possible." Evelyn looked into his face. "You're a smart man."

He laughed. "Observant, that's all."

The waitress placed their food on the table.

"Thank you," they said at the same time.

"Cracked pepper?" the waitress asked.

They both shook their heads.

"The *haus* is almost finished. The women have the garden all planned and they're ready to get on with it."

"It'll be so gut once it's done. I feel so much better. *Denke*, for all your hard work I don't know what I'd do without you. And I mean that from the bottom of my heart. You've been such a gut friend to me."

AFTER THEY'D SPENT the whole day together, they were

nearly at Beth's place. Jed stopped the buggy on the side of the road.

"What's wrong?" Evelyn asked.

He turned his body to face her. "It's what's right, and that's you and I together. I know we haven't spent much time together and you probably feel you don't know me well, but I've felt so comfortable with you that I've been able to share things with you that I haven't told anyone."

Jed took hold of her hand while Evelyn wondered if she should tell him how she felt or wait to hear what else he was going to say. She remained silent.

"Have you considered marriage a second time? I know you've got a lot happening with the *boppli* coming along at any moment …" He stared into her eyes, brought her hand to his lips and pressed his lips against it.

She pulled back in fright. Feeling as though she could hardly breathe, she said, "We should get Martha. They'll be waiting."

"I'm sorry," he said as he took up the reins.

"Nee, don't be."

Once they had collected Martha, Jed drove Martha and Evelyn home.

"Would you like to come in?" she asked when he'd pulled the buggy up at her door. She asked him in to be polite, but preferred he didn't accept so she could gather her thoughts.

"Nee denke. It's late and I should be getting back to Mark and Sally's *haus."* He helped them out of the buggy.

BECAUSE OF THEIR AWKWARD MOMENT, Evelyn had stayed

home for the next two days. When she finally went to Sally's *haus,* Sally delivered some bad news.

"What do you mean he's gone?" Evelyn stared at Sally in disbelief.

"Gone home. He said he'd go since your place is finished and it seems that Mary, his fiancée, wanted him home."

Evelyn collapsed onto the couch. Sally continued to speak, but Evelyn wasn't focused on what she was saying. All she could think of was why Jed had left. Last time she'd seen him, she'd probably given him the wrong idea —she'd pulled away from him.

Nothing made any sense, though. He told her he'd made up the story about Mary. Had she nearly become involved with another man who didn't hold much store on the truth?

"Are you okay, Evelyn?"

Evelyn wrapped both arms around her stomach, as she was gripped by pains. Her face screwed up.

Sally kneeled down beside her and put her arm around her shoulders. "Are you having contractions?"

When the pain was over, she could finally speak. "It seems so."

"I better get you home and while I'm taking you there, Mark can go fetch the midwife."

"What about Martha?"

"I'll have Mark take Martha to Beth's on the way back from the midwife."

"Denke." Evelyn did her best to put Jed out of her mind. She had lost what she'd come to think of as her one true love. Now she had to block out thoughts of Jed and concentrate on bringing her child into the world.

CHAPTER 15

"For I know the plans I have for you," declares the Lord,
*"plans to prosper you and not to harm you, plans to give you
hope and a future."*
Jeremiah 29:11

IN THE EARLY hours of the next morning, Evelyn delivered a son. Martha had a new baby brother. Evelyn laid back on the bed with her tiny son cradled in her arms. All her troubles had flown out the window. Nothing in the world mattered now—not money problems, not houses or men. The only thing that mattered was that her son had arrived and he was safe, healthy and well.

"He's perfect," Dana, the midwife stated.

"Denke, and *denke* to you too Sally for staying with me."

"Of course I'd be here for you. You'll have to be with me when I have my next one."

"Jah, I will."

101

"Whenever that will be," Sally said. "Sooner rather than later, I hope."

Evelyn kissed the top of her son's smooth bald head and stared down at his tiny features. She placed her finger against his palm and he curled his fingers tightly around it. Lowering her head against his face, she breathed in his fresh newborn scent. "There's nothing like the smell of a newborn baby."

"Let me smell." Sally leaned down and smelled the top of his head. "Mmm, freshly baked," she joked as she straightened up. "I'll go home and fetch my things and I'll be back."

"Nee, I've thought about it and I don't want you to stay. You've got your own *familye* to look after."

"You are part of my *familye.* I've got everything arranged already; you won't have to worry about a thing. I'll stay in Martha's bed for the next few days while she's at Beth's."

Evelyn looked down at her baby and kissed the top of his head once more. "I don't know what I'd do without you, Sally, but I'd rather be alone."

"That makes no sense. You should have someone here. Shouldn't she, Dana?"

The midwife replied, "There's no medical reason that you should stay, but it would be a precaution in case something were to happen."

"What could possibly happen?" Evelyn asked.

"I can't name anything off the top of my head, but bad things do happen."

"Bad things can happen at any time. I could fall down the stairs, I could accidently set the *haus* on fire, but nothing will happen. I'm on my own and I'd rather get used to it now. If it was my first, I'd love you to stay; since he's my second, I know what I'm doing."

"I can't force you I suppose. I'll come back with some meals that you can just heat up."

"That would be *wunderbaar!*"

When the midwife went downstairs, Evelyn took the opportunity to ask about Jed.

Sally answered, "I told you he's gone back to get married."

"Nee, he can't be. That can't be true."

"I know you liked him very much, but you knew all along he belonged to another. He was only here to save money."

Evelyn shook her head. "It can't have been true." The baby cried. "I'll try to feed him again."

"Looks like he's more interested this time, he's turning his head and making sucking movements with his mouth." Sally looked back at Evelyn. "Don't be so upset, you'll upset the *boppli.*"

"I'll try." Evelyn sniffed back tears.

"Everything is working out great for you. It looks like Meg and Byron Lapp want to lease your *haus.*"

"They do?"

"Jah. I was waiting for today to tell you, because you had so much on your mind yesterday."

"Denke, Sally. That does make me feel much better." Evelyn couldn't tell Sally how close she'd become to Jed, but had he lied to her? It didn't seem possible. "Sally, what do you know about the woman Jed is marrying?"

Sally sneezed. "I hope I'm not coming down with something. Jed got a call that he was needed back home.

He said his fiancée missed him. My guess is she wanted help planning the wedding."

"The women do that. What part of planning the wedding would he have needed to help with?"

"I don't know; put him out of your mind. He's gone."

She tried her best to stop the tears that stung behind her eyes, but soon they were falling down her cheeks.

"Don't cry. It's just your hormones. I don't think you're upset about Jed."

"No?"

Sally shook her head, and then mopped Evelyn's face with a damp washcloth. "You'll feel better in a day or two."

"When David was born I cried for three days straight. And not because I thought he'd be a girl. I don't know why I got so upset. I felt overwhelmed with everything— life in general." She placed the washcloth back on the nightstand and stroked her sister's shoulder. "I'll come here every day. Don't worry."

"*Denke,* Sally."

"You've got a beautiful *boppli.* What will you call him?"

"Not Tom."

Sally giggled which made Evelyn smile.

"I don't know yet. A name will come to me. I've always liked the name David. It's a strong, solid name."

"Too late," Sally said with a laugh. "You'll have to pick a more original name. We can't have two Davids in the same *familye.*"

She looked down at her baby who was nuzzling into her. "It's a shame. He looks a little like a David."

"He does actually. I'll help you think of a name. What about Nathan?"

"Jah. I like that name." She looked down at the baby. "What about Nathan David King?"

"Sounds a *wunderbaar* name to me, and David will be so pleased. He thinks he misses out on everything by being the youngest; this will be something special. I'll tell him his cousin is named for him."

"Gut. Nathan David it is, then."

"Dana said you need to have lots of fluid." She picked up the pitcher. "I'm going to fill this with water and I'll be back in a minute."

Evelyn closed her eyes, pleased that she'd soon have someone to lease the house. Amos' black horse had sold for a good price at the auction, so she would have that money for necessities in the meantime. She'd lost Jed, but she'd have a way to support her children. When she felt a little more like herself, she would contact Hezekiah and between them they could work out a payment plan so he'd get his money back.

Things weren't great but she could see that the future might be okay. Jed had changed her life by fixing her house, and she was grateful to Hezekiah for loaning Amos money. If Hezekiah hadn't loaned Amos money, Amos might have mortgaged the houses and now she'd be paying back the loan with interest to the bank. It was a standard practice amongst their Amish community that they never charged each other interest on loans made to one another.

CHAPTER 16

Trust in the Lord with all your heart
and lean not on your own understanding.
Proverbs 3:5

THE NEXT TWO days passed by in a blur. All Evelyn wanted was to get some sleep. Beth was still minding Martha.

When someone knocked on the door Evelyn opened it expecting to see Dana on her daily visit. Instead it was Mark.

"Mark! Hello." It was unusual to see Mark visiting without Sally. "Is Sally okay?"

"I'm afraid she has a bad fever."

"How bad is she?"

"Not too bad, but enough to keep her in bed. I'm afraid I'm here because I've got some bad news. Perhaps we should sit while I tell you."

"Jah, come in." She stood back to let him through the door.

When they were both sitting on the couch, he began, "It's William's old house."

Evelyn's mind went to smoke she had smelled as she was trying to sleep. She'd gotten out of bed to check that the house wasn't on fire, and when she saw that everything was okay she'd gone back to bed. But had it been William's house?

"It burned down. Not completely, but there's not much left of it.

Everything around her faded into darkness. When she came back to herself, she was on the couch with the sounds of her baby's cries ringing in her ears. She looked around and saw Mark sitting close by. He rushed to her when he saw her open her eyes.

"Evelyn, are you okay?"

"Yeah I'm okay. Did I dream about the *haus?"*

"Nee. I told you about William's *haus* and you fainted." The baby cried louder. "I haven't seen my new nephew yet. Shall I go up and fetch him for you?"

"Jah, but tell me first. How bad is it?"

He stood up. "It will need to be rebuilt."

"All that hard work you and Jed did, gone up in flames." She recalled how good the house had looked and some of the ladies in the community had even planted a garden. Now that would be all for nothing. Everyone's effort up in flames, and for what? "Why, why did this happen?" she screamed out.

Mark stood there in stunned silence.

She wished Sally was there; she would know the right

thing to say to make her feel better. How was she going to get money to live on now?

"Things will work themselves out, Evelyn," he said in a quiet voice. "I'll go and get the *boppli.*"

When he brought the baby to her, he said, "He's a fine *bu,* and he's so tiny. I forgot what they were like at this age. I almost want to keep holding him."

"He stopped crying when you picked him up, so he must like you." Evelyn held out her hands and Mark passed her the baby and sat back down.

"While you were resting, I fed the chickens and changed their water; they should be okay for a day. I'll come back and do the same again tomorrow."

"Denke." She had to feed the baby but she couldn't do so in front of Mark, and she had no desire to go back up the stairs.

"Why don't I take you to Beth's? I'd bring you all back to my place, but I wouldn't want you or the *boppli* to catch what Sally's got."

"Nee, Beth's already got Martha. The *boppli's* not much work. As long as I get some sleep tonight I'll be fine." The baby was now howling and Evelyn was jiggling him to try to keep him quiet.

"I'll be back tomorrow."

"Denke, Mark."

"And don't concern yourself with the *haus.* You get better and then we'll decide what to do."

Evelyn nodded, glad that she had Mark and Sally close by. Once Mark closed the door behind him, she leaned back on the couch and fed Nathan. She figured she'd be able to get back on top of things in a couple days.

The very next day she would go out and have a look at

how bad the house was; perhaps Mark would drive her when he came to feed the chickens. And she could see how bad things were.

That night, as though sensing her worry and torment, Nathan hardly slept. He woke up three times for feedings and then spent the rest of the time making fussy sounds in his crib. Evelyn was pleased when she woke to see the sun shining, because they were running out of clean clothes. She peeked over the side of the crib to see the baby finally asleep. She had a chance to get as many chores done as she could rather than going back to sleep.

She still hoped Mark would drive her to look at the fire-damaged house when he came to feed the chickens.

Once she had loaded the small gas-powered washing machine to capacity with bedsheets and one of her dresses, she switched it on, glad that the old machine was still working. Evelyn headed inside to fix breakfast. Although she was too tired to cook or even eat, she knew she had to keep her strength up. She fixed herself a plate of scrambled eggs, and then she headed upstairs to see if she might be able to grab a few more minutes of sleep. As soon as she was in bed with her eyes closed, her baby cried.

Evelyn rubbed her eyes and told herself she should be pleased that she'd been able to put some washing on and get some food. After she managed to get out of her comfortable bed she looked down at him. He stopped crying when she'd come close, and stared up at her.

"Hello, my *boppli*. You didn't sleep much last night; you didn't let me get much sleep either." She stretched her hands above her head and yawned. "I think you might be due for another feeding and we might have time to do that before we pin out the washing.

After the baby had been fed and the washing was on the line, she hadn't been in the house ten minutes when she heard rain. Scarcely believing her ears she looked outside to see the rain pouring down. She raced outside with a coat over her head to get her one clean dress that was on the line. When the dress was safely inside, Evelyn spread it out on a chair in front of the fire.

The sound of a buggy in the distance had Evelyn racing to the window. Each time Evelyn heard a buggy, she hoped it was Jed coming back. It was Mark's horse and buggy. She squinted to see that Mark was driving the buggy and he was alone. As he was still a fair way up the road, she took her baby in one arm and with the other she managed to slip on a clean apron. The clean apron should cover up her dress that needed washing and tomorrow if it was sunny, she could wash her other dresses.

By the time Mark pulled up at the front of the house she was ready at the front door with Nathan wrapped in a warm blanket. "Hello, Mark."

"Hello."

She hurried closer to the buggy. "Would you mind taking me to look at the *haus?*"

"Jump in. *Ach,* wait there. I'll give you a hand."

He jumped out, and took Nathan from her until she got in, and then passed him back to her.

"How's Sally today?" she asked when Mark got back into the driver's seat.

"She's better. A little better, but she's staying in bed another day. At least until the boys get back from *schul.*" He clicked the horse onward.

"That sounds like it would be a good idea."

"How are the both of you today?"

"We're fine. I'm just concerned to see how much damage the fire caused. Is the *haus* completely gone?"

"Not completely." He turned to look at her. "You scared me a little yesterday. Are you sure you're up to this?"

She nodded. "I have to be."

"I don't want to upset you."

"I won't be. I just need to know … I want to see how bad it is."

When the approached the house, all Evelyn could see was a heap of charred wood. "It's bad. It's gone. I didn't know it would be this bad." She looked over at Mark. "I thought you said some of it was okay?"

"I guess not, sorry. It's worse than I remember."

"How did the fire start? No one was living here so it couldn't have been an accident from the fireplace or a candle."

"The police suspect it was arson."

"Arson? You mean someone deliberately burned the *haus?*"

"The police said they'd come and speak with you. I told them you'd just had a baby so they said they'd wait a day or two. You were too upset for me to tell you that yesterday."

"Do they think I did it?"

"*Nee*, they just need to make a report."

"*Denke*, Mark, for talking with them and everything else you've done."

He gave an embarrassed cough and shook his head. "Was the place insured?"

"I don't think so. I haven't come across any of Amos' paperwork that says it's insured. And our *haus* isn't insured. I can't think who would've wanted to destroy the house."

"The police said it could've been youngsters—troublemakers."

"That's dreadful! What if someone had been in there?"

"They most likely knew it was vacant and that's why they did it," Mark said.

Now Evelyn had something else to worry about. Someone could set her house alight. She'd never considered that before.

She placed her baby, who was now sleeping, carefully on the seat, and then stepped down from the buggy. "Look at it, Mark, I don't think it can be rebuilt. You'd know better than me."

"It could be rebuilt. It's just whether you'd want to do that or not."

"I don't hold any special fondness for that house; it has no special memories for me. It only holds bad memories in recent times."

"Best not to mention your feelings about the house to the police until you find out if it's insured."

She glanced at Mark's face to see whether he was joking. When she saw that he wasn't, she said, "I'm positive it's not insured, but I'll go through his papers tonight to see if I can find anything." She took one last look around. "Can you take me home now?"

"Sure."

When they got back to Evelyn's house she saw the clean laundry flapping on the line. "I'm glad that rain's gone."

"What rain?"

"It rained before. Just as I put the sheets on the line."

"That's odd. It didn't rain at my place."

"It was quite a downpour."

"You'd think we would've got at least a bit of it. Anyway, I'll go and get the animal chores done for you."

"Denke, Mark."

Evelyn placed her sleeping baby in his crib and went outside to feel the sheets—they were still damp from the rain. She fetched dry sheets out of her cupboard and made her bed. There were enough diapers to last for two more days if he kept going through as many as he had been. If the next day wasn't sunny, she'd still have to do washing and pin everything on the covered line in the barn to dry.

She headed back downstairs to see if Mark wanted a cup of tea. When she opened the front door, Mark was walking up the steps with a bucket of eggs.

"There you are," he said as he handed them to her.

"I completely forgot to fetch the eggs. Martha and I normally do it together of a morning."

"You can't do everything. Do you need anything else? I've given the stall a quick clean. I'll give it a better going over tomorrow, and I've given the horse and the chickens fresh water."

"Nee, that's fine, *denke.* Go home and look after Sally."

CHAPTER 17

Do not conform any longer to the pattern of this world, but be
transformed by the renewing of your mind.
Then you will be able to test and approve what
God's will is—his good, pleasing and perfect will.
Romans 12:2

As soon as Mark left, Evelyn placed the eggs in the container in the kitchen. Now with the baby asleep, she would have a peaceful and quiet cup of tea. When she turned on the tap to fill the pot, the tap came off in her hand and the water sprang up like a fountain. She tried her best to screw it back on with water hitting her in the face, but it wouldn't fit. Remembering there was a water main switch outside, she got the wrench out from under the sink and hurried outside. She finally located the water main and turned it off.

Now soaking wet, she had to get out of her clothes;

she couldn't afford to get sick. She squeezed as much water as she could out of her dress and headed upstairs. There were no clean dresses left, so she changed into her nightgown, put her dressing gown over it, and went back downstairs. Evelyn mopped up the kitchen floor while trying her best to keep herself as dry as she could. Once the area was dry, she studied the tap and the broken section. She could see that she'd have to keep the water to the house switched off until it was repaired. With a heavy sigh, she pulled her boots on, and then collected all the containers she could find to fill up with water from the rainwater tank. The tank was mainly used for the livestock.

When she'd carted water inside, she recalled Mark said that the police might visit her. She couldn't answer the door in her dressing gown; a clean apron would have to disguise the fact that her dress wasn't clean.

When she pulled out her drawer and saw that this was the last clean one, she was upset. *I must be thankful that I do have a clean apron,* she thought trying to keep herself focused on staying positive. Evelyn was totally exhausted once she'd changed again.

Right then, Nathan woke and cried. She picked him up. "I'll feed you down by the fire so we'll be warmer."

Once they got down the stairs, she saw the fire was dying. She carefully propped the baby on the couch and placed another log on the fire.

By the time she'd finished feeding her son, there was a nice fire burning. She lifted Nathan upright and stared into his eyes. "I hope you know how much I love you. It won't always be this hectic. Things will calm down." Without warning, vomit shot out of the baby's mouth.

She looked down at her no-longer-clean apron. "Why didn't I know that was just about to happen?" Once again, she propped the baby between pillows, wiped his mouth with a clean section of her apron and headed to clean herself up.

"Anybody home?"

Evelyn heard Beth's voice, calling out from the front door. "Come in, Beth." She'd forgotten that Martha would be coming home today. Evelyn met them at the door.

"I can't stay, I'm in a hurry," Beth said.

"Don't you want to see the *boppli?*"

Beth raised her eyebrows. "Of course. Where is he?"

"He's on the couch. Can't you stay a little while?" Evelyn wanted to share her dreadful day with someone.

"Nee." Beth stood over the baby. "He's so sweet."

Evelyn looked at Martha who was looking glum with her arms folded. "What's wrong with you, Martha?"

"Martha's cross because she wanted to stay and play with Jemima."

"I didn't want to come home. There's no one to play with here."

"This is where you live; you have to come home. The baby and I need you."

"I must go," Beth said.

"Okay. *Denke* for watching her."

Evelyn closed the front door once Beth was back in her buggy.

"I want to stay with Jemima."

"You can play with her another time. You've got your *bruder* to play with."

Martha pouted. "He's too little."

117

"When he's bigger you can play with him, but it's true, right now he's too tiny."

"Can't I go back to Jemima?"

"Nee! And you can go to bed right now if you keep asking me the same question over and over. You've been told you can play with Jemima another time, but not today." Realizing she'd never spoken so harshly to her daughter, she added, "You must be *gut* today. It won't be long before you can play with your *bruder.*"

"How long?"

"In a few months. You'll be able to sing to him, and tell him stories."

"Is that long?" Martha asked.

"It'll go quickly."

"When can I play with him?"

Evelyn groaned; she was not in the mood for a grumpy child when she was barely holding things together. "The time will go quicker if you stop asking about it."

"Why?"

"Because that's the way things are."

"But why?" Martha's voice was turning into whining the more she spoke.

"Martha! Stop it! I can't take any more!" Evelyn shouted.

Martha's mouth fell open and she stared at her mother with large round eyes. It was the first time that Evelyn had raised her voice at her child. She didn't know what to do. She considered apologizing but she couldn't recall a time when her parents had apologized to her when she was a child.

"Go and find something to play with and leave me alone for just a moment."

When a knock sounded on the door Evelyn was pleased. *This will be Beth. Sounds like she's changed her mind about staying for a chat. Maybe she'll offer to take Martha for another day.* She opened the door to see two uniformed police officers.

"Good day, Ma'am," said the taller one, who was standing closest to the door.

"Hello."

"Are you Evelyn King?"

"Yes, have you come about the house?"

They nodded.

"My brother-in-law said you'd be coming by. Come in." She stepped back to let them pass. "Martha, go and play with your toys."

Martha stomped to the corner of the room and sat with her toys. She mostly played with wooden blocks and other toys that Amos' *vadder* had made for her.

After Evelyn scooped her baby into her arms, she said, "Perhaps we should sit in the kitchen. It's this way."

Once they were seated, the tall officer pulled out a notepad and pen. Evelyn was instantly itchy and knew her nerve rash was back. She looked down at her hands holding Nathan to see that they were shaking.

"Cute baby," the quieter of the two said.

"He's only a few days old." She tried to hide her trembling hands under the baby's blanket.

"You seem to be nervous, Mrs. King; why's that?" the tall one asked.

"I *am* nervous. My brother-in-law said that you think the fire might have been lit deliberately and I'm hoping you don't think I did it."

"Did you?" the other one leaned in to ask.

"No. I didn't. That's the only money I had to live on. Well, it would've been when it was leased. It's only just been fixed up. It was in a dreadful condition before that."

"Was it insured?" the taller officer asked, ready to jot down his notes.

"No. I'm sure it wasn't. But I still haven't been through all my husband's things."

"Yes, we heard about your husband. We're sorry for your loss."

"Yes, we are," the short officer added.

Evelyn nodded. "It came as a shock. It was an aneurism. Which I knew nothing about until Amos' father died six months before of the very same thing." *Stop talking so much,* she told herself. She tried to steady her nerves by deep breathing. "The last thing I wanted was for anything to happen to the house."

"We believe you."

"You do?"

They both nodded, but that didn't stop them from staying for fifteen more minutes and asking many probing questions.

When they left, Evelyn was unbelievably exhausted. If she hadn't had Martha there, she would've had tried to get some sleep.

She sat down on the couch holding Nathan who was nearly asleep.

"Can you open the toy box for me?" Martha asked her mother.

The lid on the wooden box was far too heavy for a girl Martha's age to open.

"Okay, if you'll ask properly." After Martha did so, Evelyn stood up. She laid Nathan on the couch and propped pillows on his side, even though he was far too young to roll over by himself.

When Evelyn opened the toy box, a large spider sprang out at her. Evelyn jumped back screaming. Then she pulled Martha back.

"Go and sit on the lounge by your *bruder*." She picked up a block of wood to hit the spider with. If Amos had been there she would've had him catch the spider and release it outside so it wouldn't be killed. After all, a spider had a right to live. But with no one else there, it seemed like it was either her or the spider.

Just then Hezekiah threw open her door. "I heard screams. Are you all right?"

"There's a spider!" Martha shouted as she jumped up and down.

Hezekiah jumped into action. "Where did it go?"

"I think it went under there." Evelyn pointed to the blanket Martha had been sitting on.

He turned to Evelyn. "Do you have a container?"

"You're not going to kill it?" Evelyn asked.

"Not if I don't have to."

"I'll get one." Evelyn hurried to the kitchen, pleased that Hezekiah thought the same way as she about spiders. Most people would've squashed the spider and thought nothing of it.

Once he'd successfully captured the spider, he took it outside. Evelyn collapsed onto the couch, lifting Nathan into one arm and snuggling Martha close to her side with the other. Could God be giving her a sign that Hezekiah was the man she should marry? Jed had gone, but it seemed like Hezekiah would always be around to look after her. He was kind and caring even though he was older. Perhaps an older man, and one who'd been married before, would make a better husband than a man who traveled around with no cares.

Hezekiah walked back in with the empty container.

"Can you put it in the kitchen?"

When he came back into the living room, he sat down and lifted up the broken tap. "How long has your kitchen been like that?"

"The tap?"

He nodded.

"A few weeks now. I've been collecting water from the tank."

"I'll have it fixed today. All it needs is the broken section replaced and a new tap. Evelyn, why didn't you tell me of this?"

"I didn't want to bother you."

"I offered to do things for you. It would make me happy to do things for you."

"*Denke,* Hezekiah."

Martha smiled at him as she stood next to him looking at him.

"I'll go to the hardware store and pick a few things up and I'll have it fixed in no time."

"You can do that?"

He nodded. "Do you need anything while I'm out?"

She shook her head. *"Nee,* I don't." *Some sleep!*

While Hezekiah was away, she had a good think about her situation. Her sister was right; if she married Hezekiah she'd never have to worry about anything. He was a solid reliable man and a capable and caring person. He'd already chopped her wood and chased a spider out of the house, and now he was fixing her tap. Hezekiah was there when she needed him and where was Jed? Jed was nowhere to be seen just the same as Amos had always been. She couldn't carry on without help—she needed a man who'd be there all the time—a man with whom she could have a real family.

CHAPTER 18

The thief comes only to steal and kill and destroy; I have come
that they may have life,
and have it to the full.
John 10:10

"MR. HOSTER BACK NOW, *MAMM.*"

"*Denke* for letting me know." By the time Hezekiah returned, the baby was asleep upstairs. It meant a great deal to have her tap fixed. Now she wouldn't have to go out into the cold and bring water inside every day.

Martha and Evelyn watched as Hezekiah replaced the tap and the broken connection.

"I didn't know you could do things like that, Hezekiah."

"I can do all kinds of things," he said smiling.

"Well, now I can offer you a cup of tea."

"Jah please." He looked down at his hands. "I'll put my tools back in the buggy and wash up outside."

"Can I go with you?" Martha asked in a tiny voice.

"Okay," Hezekiah said.

It hadn't escaped Evelyn's notice that Martha was very fond of Hezekiah. She rubbed her tired eyes as she filled the pot with water. Having a husband by her side is something that she needed right now. Feeling warm fuzzy gooiness and feeling butterflies over a man meant nothing if the man wasn't there when she needed him. She said she'd only marry a second time for love, but that wasn't practical. Now she had two children to raise; she had to put her fancies aside and be practical. Her children needed a stable father they could look up to—Hezekiah was that man.

She looked out the window at her daughter holding Hezekiah's hand as they headed back to the house. It warmed her heart to see the affection Martha had for him already, and he seemed to return it.

Once she made the tea, she gave Martha cookies in a bowl and sat her by her toys in the living room. She wanted to speak to Hezekiah in private. Martha was happy to eat the cookies in the living room as she normally was allowed only one cookie a day, and now she had two in her bowl.

She placed the tea in front of Hezekiah and sat down next to him. "Hezekiah, I've been thinking about what you asked me recently."

"About marrying me?"

She nodded. "My answer is yes."

His face lighted up. "You will marry me?"

"I will."

"That pleases me." He took her hand and squeezed it gently.

"Me too."

"We should get married soon."

"Okay," she agreed.

"I must go now. I've got people waiting on me to tell them what to do with the next job. I'll come back and see you soon to talk about when to speak to the bishop."

Evelyn looked down at the tea she'd just made him. He hadn't said he was in a hurry when she'd made it. When he stood, she stood too. "I'll walk you out."

When he was gone, Evelyn sat in front of the fire. Marrying Hezekiah seemed the only reasonable choice she could make. He'd shown he was a reliable man and that's the kind of husband she needed; she was too tired to raise two children on her own.

WHEN EVELYN GOT into bed that night, she tried to push her worries aside. Surely things would be better when she married Hezekiah. Just like the widow in the bible, she'd taken a step in faith when she'd agreed to marry Hezekiah. In the back of her mind, she heard a tiny voice telling her she was making the same mistake twice. She'd married Amos without loving him and now she was marrying Hezekiah without being in love with him. But if she didn't marry Hezekiah, what would become of her?

She closed her eyes and prayed. *I put my life in your hands, God. I'll trust that you'll provide for me and my kinner; please help me trust more, and please give me more faith so I can trust you without doubting.* Immediately, Evelyn felt better. *We don't live in tomorrow we live in today,* she reminded herself.

Evelyn slept soundly most of that night. She only had to wake once to feed the baby.

The next morning there was a knock on her door just as she was fixing Martha breakfast. She opened the door expecting to see Sally or Mark at such an early hour.

"Jed!" As soon as she saw him she had a dreadful feeling in the pit of her stomach. She'd made a huge mistake agreeing to marry Hezekiah. She stepped aside to let him in.

"I'm sorry I had to leave so quickly days ago. I called Mary to see how she was and she was in tears. Her parents were trying to make her marry another man, since I had left. I had to go and sort the situation out. In the end, I think disaster was averted." He looked around and laughed. "Look at you! You look *wunderbaar,* and Sally tells me you've had the *boppli.*"

"He's asleep at the moment. He's a beautiful *bu.* I called him Nathan."

"That's a fine name. I'm anxious to see him."

Now that he was here, she knew that her heart belonged to him. She would have to tell Hezekiah that she had changed her mind. "Come and sit down on the couch and warm up by the fire." When they both were seated, she said, "You saved your friend from having to marry someone?"

"*Jah,* I did. I had a good talk with her parents too, along with Mary. We both told them the truth of how we were pretending there was something between us so Mary wouldn't feel pressured. I think they understood and they said they would stop trying to marry her off."

"The truth is always the best." Now she knew she'd have to tell him that, while he was gone and she didn't think he'd return, she'd agreed to marry Hezekiah. She hoped he'd understand.

"So in the end, the result was good all around. Mary and I don't have to pretend anymore, and I've helped Mary avoid a disastrous marriage."

"Then you'd agree that marrying the wrong person would be a disaster?"

"Jah it would. That's why I haven't married up until now." He took hold of her hand. "Evelyn, I have something to ask you."

She stared into his blue eyes, and with him it just felt right.

A knock on the door interrupted them.

"You stay there, I'll get it." He opened the door to see Hezekiah.

"Jed! I didn't expect to see you here in this *haus."*

"I came to visit Evelyn and the new baby."

Hezekiah looked over his shoulder at Evelyn seated on the couch. "Have you told him our news, Evelyn?"

This was the worst thing that could've happened. All she could do was put both hands to her mouth and stare at the two of them. She was certain Jed had been just about to ask her to marry him. She'd made the biggest mistake of her life agreeing to marry Hezekiah.

When she remained silent, Jed looked back at Hezekiah. "News? What news is that?"

"Evelyn and I are to be married," Hezekiah announced.

CHAPTER 19

*I am not ashamed: for I know whom I have believed, and am
persuaded that he is able to keep
that which I have committed unto him against that day.*
2 Timothy 1:12

JED TOOK A STEP BACK. He turned and stared at Evelyn taking a step toward her. "It's not true, is it?"

Evelyn looked into his eyes feeling as though her heart was breaking into pieces. If only he hadn't left when he did. Why hadn't he stayed? Wasn't she more important than a childhood friend?

"Hezekiah asked me …"

"And you said yes?"

Hezekiah answered for her. "Evelyn has agreed to marry me."

Jed hadn't looked at Hezekiah when he'd spoken; his

eyes had remained fixed on Evelyn. "Is that why you made that comment to me just now about the wrong person?"

Evelyn frowned as she tried to recall what she'd said. "I'm not certain." After she spoke Evelyn recalled she had asked him if he would agreed that marrying the wrong person would be a disaster. It was a possibility that Jed thought she was telling him that marrying him would be a disaster. "I wasn't meaning you," she finally added.

"Congratulations on your new *boppli*, Evelyn, and congratulations to both of you on your happy news. Good day to you both." And with that, he walked straight past Hezekiah and out the door.

Hezekiah sat down next to her. "What was he talking about?"

"I'm not certain; my head is a bit fuzzy—I've been so tired since Nathan's come along."

"It took Jane months to get back to normal after each birth."

Evelyn held her head in her hands. What was she going to do? She'd agreed to marry Hezekiah as a way out of her problems, but that was no basis for a marriage. Not the kind of marriage she'd had dreams of, at least. How could she let this kind man down in a gentle way? Even if things with her and Jed would never be the same she knew that she couldn't marry Hezekiah while she had feelings in her heart for another man.

"We shouldn't marry, Evelyn."

She looked up at him stunned. "What do you mean?"

"Do you have to ask me that?"

Embarrassment burned her cheeks and she could no longer look at him.

"I can see it all over your face. It's that man, Jed, you care about and not me."

She looked back at him. "I do care about you, Hezekiah."

He chuckled. "But not in the same way. It seems you have a great deal of affection for that man and that is why we cannot marry."

Even though what he said was true, part of her felt it was another rejection— another let down for her — another loss.

"*Denke* for being so kind understanding. You're a remarkable man."

"I'll still be around to help you with anything that needs doing."

All she wanted to do right now was cry and be alone. She put her hand on her forehead. "I think I need to have a bit of a sleep now. Sally or Mark will drop by later to see if I need anything. They always come by."

Hezekiah left the house quietly, and then she was alone again.

Why did everything have to be so hard? Evelyn had watched all her older sisters get married, and have children and perfect families. On top of that, her sisters had been in love with their husbands before they'd married. In her heart, she knew that things with Jed would never be the same. As soon as he was gone for a few days, she'd already moved on. How could a man recover from a betrayal like that?

With both Hezekiah and Jed out of her life she had many things to consider. What if she sold the house to Hezekiah? The burned-down house and land in exchange for wiping the debt? It seemed like a good idea if Hezekiah would be agreeable to it.

She hadn't heard Hezekiah leave, so she hurried to the window to see that Hezekiah was only just climbing into his buggy. She opened the door and waved him back.

He headed toward her.

"I just had a thought. I don't know if you'll be agreeable to it, but in exchange for my debt to you, would you be willing to have the fire-damaged *haus* and my *vadder*-in-law's land?"

He tipped his hat slightly back on his head to scratch the top of his hairline. "Would you be willing to do that?"

"I figured the land wouldn't be worth much more than that figure."

"The land could be worth a great deal more than that. I'll look into things and I would be willing to pay you the going rate, less the debt."

"Denke; that would be a burden taken off my shoulders, but only if it works out for you too."

He smiled at her, nodded and walked back to his buggy. Evelyn was pleased that he didn't seem to be holding any resentment toward her. Without the second house, her hopes for an income from it would be gone, but at least it was getting rid of a debt. And she wouldn't have to worry over what to do with the burned-ßdown house.

She'd been a fool to panic and say she would marry Hezekiah. She'd fallen into the same trap as she had when she agreed to marry Amos—she was marrying out of convenience and desperation—not love. Seeing Jed again had given her strength.

Scratching her stomach, she could feel her nerve-rash

coming back. What would Jed think of her now? He would think, *you're an opportunistic woman marrying a wealthy man just so he could give you a comfortable lifestyle.* She'd ruined things between herself and Jed, and now he'd most likely gone back home. Jed had to have come there to ask her to marry him. What a big fool she'd been.

With God's strength, she decided she'd make a life for her children and herself. She'd write a list of what was wrong with her house and all her brother-in-laws could do a little bit each to help. Was it pride that had stopped her asking for help in the past? While she was at it, she decided to be on the lookout for ways to help others and not be so consumed with her own problems.

Martha ran to her from the kitchen and climbed on the couch beside her. *"Dat* gone, *Mamm?"*

Still not knowing whether she meant her father or Hezekiah, Evelyn smiled and put her arm around her. "He's gone, Martha. He's gone home."

Right then both of them jumped as their front door was flung open. They turned to see Jed.

CHAPTER 20

Yea, though I walk through the valley of the shadow of death, I will fear no evil: for thou art with me; thy rod and thy staff they comfort me.
Psalm 23:4

"As soon as I got back to Mark's *haus,* I knew I had to come back to see you. That comment you made got me thinking. Do you remember what it was?"

Martha ran to him.

Evelyn said, "Excuse me, Jed, for a moment. Martha, come and play with your toys here on the blanket."

"I want to play with Mr. Esh."

"Nee! It's adults' time to talk. You sit down."

"Okay, *Mamm."*

Evelyn looked back at Jed. "We can talk in the kitchen."

He followed her into the kitchen and, as she picked up the pot, he said, "I don't want tea or anything else. I've come back to make sure that you're not making a big mistake. Will you sit?"

She stared at him, wondering if he traveled around the countryside trying to save women from marrying the wrong men. Was she just a friend to him as Mary was? He'd helped Mary get out of an unsuitable marriage —was he trying to save her from a marriage to Hezekiah?

When she sat down, he cleared his throat, and then said, "Evelyn, I came here earlier today to ask you to marry me."

She gulped.

"Then I found out you were marrying Hezekiah. Why had you never mentioned that you were involved with the man? With all the time we'd spent together and how things were between us, I thought we had something."

"I thought so too. Hezekiah asked me all of a sudden."

"Are you in love with the man?"

She shook her head. *"Nee!* I'm not!"

"Then, why are you marrying him, Evelyn?"

"I'm not. I told him, or rather, he told me when you left this morning … he said it was clear who I had feelings for and it wasn't him."

"Did he mean me?"

She laughed. *"Jah."*

"So you're not going to marry him?"

"Nee!"

He leaned forward and grabbed her hand. "Evelyn, will you marry me?"

She looked into his eyes and all she could do was nod. She couldn't speak.

He laughed and wiped a tear from his eye. "Were you

ever going to tell me your engagement to Hezekiah was off, or just wait for me to find out for myself?"

"I don't know what I was doing. I'm sorry I agreed to marry Hezekiah—it was thoughtless and silly. I didn't know you'd be coming back. You just disappeared and it reminded me of Amos."

"I didn't mean for that to happen. The last time I saw you I thought you were a little distant with me, and I thought time apart might be good for both of us—I guess that's why I didn't tell you I was going."

"It's one of those potholes of life we talked about some time ago."

Jed nodded. "A large one. I'm sorry I did that to you. I never want you to feel like I've deserted you. I'll do my best to make you feel safe."

"I'm so tired of worrying about things all the time. I'm so tired in general." Evelyn tried to stop the tears but she couldn't. A stream of tears flowed down her cheeks.

Jed stood and moved his chair beside hers. He put his arm around her and she rested her head on his shoulder. "I'm here now to take care of you and Martha, and my new son that I haven't even met yet."

Evelyn laughed. "Don't make me wake him. I need a rest."

"I won't. I've plenty of time."

She wiped tears from her eyes but stayed resting against his shoulder. "Where will we live?"

"You're not worried about things already are you?" he joked.

She smiled. "I don't care where we live."

"We can live where ever you want to live. I have a business in Ohio, a lumberyard, but it can run without me and

I can live here. I could even open a second one here." He looked around him at the house. "We can buy a new *haus*, or make this one bigger."

She looked into his eyes. "Do you have the money to do that?"

He nodded. "We can rebuild William's house. I heard about it burning down. I say 'William' as if I knew him, but I never knew your *vadder*-in-law."

"I have offered Hezekiah that he can buy it to wipe out the debt Amos left."

"Amos had a debt?"

"He hadn't told me, but he'd been out of work for the past year and regularly borrowed money from Hezekiah, probably so I wouldn't find out he'd lost his job."

"It's a hard thing for a man to face not being able to provide for his family."

She looked into his eyes and when he smiled back at her she knew that to start anew she had to tell him all of all her concerns. She sat straight. "I need to tell you some things about the marriage I had with Amos. It wasn't what it seemed to other people."

"You did tell me you weren't in love with him, and you told me he was away from the house a lot."

"It was more than that. I just want you to know so you know the things that upset me and things that I might be sensitive about." She shared with him all the things that had happened—and had not happened—between her and Amos and how he didn't pay her or Martha much attention.

"It won't be like that with us, Evelyn. It won't be like that at all. I've always wanted *kinner*. And I won't be leaving you to spend my time at another *haus*."

She stared into his eyes and knew that it was true.

"If we decide to stay here, I don't want you to live in this *haus* anymore, and I prefer you to sell the other house to Hezekiah. I want us to start brand-new with everything."

"Can we have a house where no spiders can get in?"

He laughed. "I'll try everything I can to keep them out, and if one does come in I'll make certain it's not in the house very long. How does that sound?"

"That sounds fine to me." She laughed and rested her head on his shoulder again.

There were still so many unanswered questions—how William's house had burned down, how Martha would adjust to a new father, and a dozen other things, but wasn't life always like that? Not knowing everything all at once had caused Evelyn many a nerve-rash. Just like the widow from the Bible, she'd trust. From today, she would choose to trust in God and believe that no matter if things looked bad, God would turn things around—even in the very last hour.

Who knoweth not in all these that
the hand of the LORD hath wrought this?
Job 12:9

≈

Thank you for your interest in
Amish Widow's Proposal.

To be first to learn of Samantha Price's new releases, and receive special offers, join her email list on the 'mailing list' section of her website: www.samanthapriceauthor.com

All books in the EXPECTANT AMISH WIDOWS series.

Book 1 Amish Widow's Hope

Book 2 The Pregnant Amish Widow

Book 3 Amish Widow's Faith

Book 4 Their Son's Amish Baby

Book 5 Amish Widow's Proposal

Book 6 The Pregnant Amish Nanny

Book 7 A Pregnant Widow's Amish Vacation

Book 8 The Amish Firefighter's Widow

Book 9 Amish Widow's Secret

Book 10 The Middle-Aged Amish Widow

Book 11 Amish Widow's Escape

Book 12 Amish Widow's Christmas

Book 13 Amish Widow's New Hope

Book 14 Amish Widow's Story

Book 15 Amish Widow's Decision

Book 16 Amish Widow's Trust

Book 17 The Amish Potato Farmer's Widow

≈

ABOUT THE AUTHOR

Samantha Price is a best selling author who knew she wanted to become a writer at the age of seven, while her grandmother read to her Peter Rabbit in the sun room. Though the adventures of Peter and his sisters Flopsy, Mopsy, and Cotton-tail started Samantha on her creative journey, it is now her love of Amish culture that inspires her to write. Her writing is clean and wholesome, with more than a dash of sweetness. Though she has penned over eighty Amish Romance and Amish Mystery books, Samantha is just as in love today with exploring the spiritual and emotional journeys of her characters as she was the day she first put pen to paper. Samantha lives in a quaint Victorian cottage with three rambunctious dogs.

www.samanthapriceauthor.com
  samanthaprice333@gmail.com
  www.facebook.com/SamanthaPriceAuthor
  Follow Samantha Price on BookBub
  Twitter @ AmishRomance

29104642R00082

Made in the USA
San Bernardino, CA
11 March 2019